Glenn Gould

Light and Dark

a novel

by

John Passfield

Rock's Mills Press

Rock's Mills, Ontario • Oakville, Ontario

2023

Cover Illustration: John Passfield
Cover Design: Craig Passfield

Author's Website: www.johnpassfield.ca

For information, including permissions and bulk/retail purchases, please contact the publisher at customer.service@rocksmillspress.com.

Chapter 1

Sitting at the piano. I am in Washington D. C. At the Phillip's Gallery.
A single spotlight shining down from the skies above.

It is my American musical debut. I am wearing a dark business suit. I am eschewing the white tie and tails. You are not meeting just another prodigy. You are experiencing Glenn Gould – for the very first time. Not a lot of people in the house. A hundred and fifty at best. But some of the most important minds in music today. The bushes have been beaten – the word has been relayed. You don't want to miss this kid – he sure knows how to play. I have chosen my program carefully. Gibbons – Sweelinck – Bach. Beethoven – Berg – Webern. I know what I want to convey. The shuffling stops. Full calm. I take my hand out of my pocket. I start to play.

One of these times,

Newspaper articles hailing a young phenomenon.
A poster advertising a rising star.
A young stripling coming out on stage.

I will write my autobiography –

What is it like to read a book about yourself?
A sense, perhaps, that a vandal has ransacked your home?
What compelled you to write a critical review?

which will certainly be fiction.

A stagehand adjusting the height of a piano.
A young boy wearing a hat and winter gloves.
An audience getting restless in their seats.

New York. The Town Hall.
Fingers flying in a blur across a keyboard.

The word has spread like wildfire. The telephone wires have been humming a tune. You gotta hear this kid from Canada. A bit of a kook, but he sure knows how to play. A small hall and a small crowd. But some of the most powerful musical mandarins of the day. Benefactors – patrons – publishers. A number of pianists as well. I work my magic at the keyboard. The same pieces as I played in Washington – played in the same Glenn-Gould way. The applause is overwhelming. An encore at intermission. A hundred people backstage. A party for me in Manhattan with every music-aficionado here. Everyone crowding around in praise of the musical find. I feign an upset stomach and leave just as soon as I can.

He was a phenomenon who came out of nowhere. His debut was auspicious in the extreme. The stars were in full alignment. An ominous silence filled the hall. There was not one cough or sneeze as he started to play.

"Glenn Gould is the greatest thing that has happened to music in years."
"In the world of music, Glenn Gould shines like a radiant beacon."

"What a spell-binding performer. The slim carriage – the shock of unruly hair. The rickety chair – the nonchalance. The absence of the traditional tie and tails. They say this young boy is barely out of his teens. Taking his place – raising his hands – the audience leaning forward in anticipation. And the music – Oh my, the music! A revelation when this young man starts to play. Who knew that Bach could be played in just this way? I tell you, I thought of an angel, and I'm not all that religious. So young – so slim – so beautiful. A radiant musical angel – bringing sounds down to earth that have not been heard. Every line of every fugue so clear and so clean. And the fingers seeming to fly above the keys. Oh, I tell you I couldn't sleep for days – not for days after hearing this young man play."

Sitting at the piano - thought of an angel - other musicians looked askance - rolling in like the tide - works that are not played - a footprint in the sand - a musical parasite - to liquefy yourself - write at the highest level - any sort of life.

People are writing about me constantly. But most of the time they don't have any idea what they're talking about. Very few of them ever come near the true Glenn Gould.

Oh, I'm not saying that an accurate biography cannot be written. No, that is far from any implication that I wish to proffer. A certain kind of person lends himself well to a traditional biography, no doubt.

No, what I am saying is that my story cannot be easily told. Where to start? – where to end? – what to squeeze in-between? And those who try will get little help from me.

Suddenly, they were standing in the midst of a carnival.
Right next to them was a whirling merry-go-round.
The organ played the familiar circus tune.

A coffee shop in Manhattan. My dad, my manager and me. They have coffee while I drink bottled water. In reserve is a carton of skim milk which I brought along.

A handsome young pianist on the cover of a magazine.

The New York newspapers spread on the table. The New York Times and the New York Herald-Tribune. Nothing but praise for the kid from up North. 'Complete enthralment' – 'other-worldly' – 'depths of feeling and perception'. My dad reads one review and I read another. 'Mesmerizing' – 'thrilled' – 'sensitively poetic' – 'fragile nuance' – 'beauty and significance'. My manager smiles and reads another one. 'A rare gift for the world'. Exactly what I was aiming at. Well worth the rent that I had to pay for the hall.

There was a man who lived in Frankfort. He was about to embark on the life of an engineer. He knew how to tie his tie and what gloves to wear. A little out-of-sorts, but otherwise fine. Could he afford to spend three weeks breathing mountain air?

Preparing for my debut at the cottage.
Flying down to Washington and New York.

"People are already comparing him to the iconic young men of the day. The arrogant swagger of Marlon Brando. The poetic reticence of James Dean. The essential innocence of a young Montgomery Clift. Those photos on the album cover. The latest idol to burst on the scene. The iconoclastic rebel against the old fogeys of a bygone musical era. The quotable quips of the multiple interviews. The brash self-confidence and bold audacity of his liner-notes. Coming out of nowhere – the backwoods of Canada – and claiming his place at the apex of the culture. Making himself the creative partner – the co-creator – of the venerable Bach. A young King Arthur of infinite promise – waving the sword which was lodged in the stone. Pianist – composer – critic – record-producer – engineer. As futuristic in theory as a McLuhan or an Ennis. As classically-rooted as the great Beethoven himself. Roll the red carpet right down the middle of Fifth Avenue. This lad has not one pot-hole in his path."

The larger musical web - under the microscope - the loneliest animal -
the anti-facts - exploring every topic - penetrated their bones - the alternative
to control - the soil of winter - glowing radio dial - he's had a vision.

They'll have to stretch their minds a bit – a whole lot in fact – to encompass everything that a life like mine has to offer. And it won't be only the music – 'On such and such a date, Glenn Gould played such and such a piece of music – on the piano – in the key of G.' No, they'll have to do much more than to list the dates and the events.

I must confess that I am an inveterate reader of the biographies of other people. Music-biography has always been my secret vice. A diabetic with a box of chocolates on a lonely night.

Let's see – there's Mozart, Beethoven, Schoenberg, Strauss and many, many more. Over the years, I've read the biographies of them all. By far the best life that I am aware of is the life of Bach.

*The food piled up
in the royal granary.*

An office in mid-town Manhattan.
A man whose face is obscured by the smoke of a big cigar.
I tell ya, I was lucky I was there last night. It was Schneider who gave me the tip. Said there's a boy coming down from Canada – plays like nobody else can play. That's the only reason I was sitting in the hall. I could barely believe my ears. I couldn't believe the amount of control – the way you separated the voices. I knew that I'd made a major find. I looked around for the other publishers. I told myself I'd call your manager the very next day. You can read the contract carefully – every t and every i. Carte blanche for choice of material. Generous terms if I may so say. You know, this is certainly unprecedented. At least as far as memory serves. Never before have we given a contract to anyone in music after only one performance in this town. That makes you quite unique. I think this calls for a toast. I've got a little something here in my desk. You're going to have a fairy-tale career.

Bach: The Goldberg Variations / Goldberg Variations / Beethoven: Piano Sonatas Nos. 30-32 / Piano Sonata No. 30 / Piano Sonata No. 31 / Piano Sonata No. 32 / Bach: Concerto No. 1 in D minor, BWV 1052 & Beethoven: Concerto No. 2 in B-flat major, Op. 19 / Bach: Concerto No. 1 in D minor, BWV 1052 / Beethoven: Piano Concerto No. 2 / Bach: Partitas Nos. 5 & 6; Fugues in F-sharp minor and E major / Partita No. 5 in G major, BWV 829 / Partita No. 6 in E minor, BWV 830 / Fugue No. 9 in E major, BWV 878 / Fugue No. 14 in F-sharp minor, BWV 883 /

My theory of the future of music is very simple. It will arrive as the leaves will appear on the trees. It will be a natural outgrowth of the present, as the present is a natural outgrowth of earlier days. The future, in embryonic form, is available to us now. I only want to enjoy what is ours to enjoy.

Loud chatter by patrons in a lobby.

A reporter filing his story on a telephone.
Intense applause as a young man enters a room.

The artist-spokesman's role \ invent a form \ managed to typecast yourself \ a contrapuntal instrument \ a validity or lack of validity \ strands are leitmotivically controlled \ minute musical connections \ the composer-performer relationship \ the relevant criterion \ a perfect musical analogy.

What balance of music and life do you think would be best?
Is the music entirely separate from the life?
Or are the music and the life inseparably entwined?

A boy was born in a suburb of Toronto.

Taxis pulling up to a major venue.
A newsboy shouting news of the latest sensation.
A crowd lining up for a major event.

Certainly I am a hypochondriac. This has always been my contention. There are those who think my hypochondria is amazingly robust, and there are those who feel that my hypochondria – though real – is rather anaemic, considering the forces at play wherein my health is concerned. If one were to follow me around for a day or so – which I would never allow, by the way – noting my aches, my pains, my consumption of pills, my realistic and my imaginary fears, one might well be able to formulate – anecdotal though it might be – a reasonably-accurate picture of the general state of my health.

East 30th Street in New York. A beautiful old church. The best recording equipment in the world. All the best engineers at my beck and call.
A bank of turning tape recorders on a studio wall.
A sound board and a tall thermos of coffee. An older, tired-looking man. Says here you want the Goldberg. You know that's already been done? Most people think of the harpsichord. Pretty early in your career. Don't you think you'd better start out with something else? The Two-Part Inventions would make a good entry-level choice. No, I'd rather do the Goldberg. He pauses for a while. He is thinking it over slowly – not meeting my eyes. I am about to mention the contract – remind him that I have been given carte blanche. He sighs and I see just the hint of a smile. He looks up and the smile gets bigger. Hey, what the heck – why not? Let's take a chance. After all, this is going to be your career.

There was a man who lived in Tokyo. He was a painter but he could not paint in the city. The city offered no topics for his art. He sought a quiet inn in a tranquil countryside. Surely there he would find a subject which was fit to paint.

"Glenn Gould has nothing like the technique of a young Horowitz."

"The incomparable Backhaus is undoubtedly closer to the Beethoven poetry."

"I don't know what it is, but it isn't music. He acts, when he is on stage, like a petulant child. He has absolutely no respect for the other musicians. His contempt for them exudes from his every pore. He crosses his legs and looks at the ceiling when he is awaiting his turn to play. He gestures to the stage-hands about an imaginary draught. And wearing that coat and gloves as he's waiting in the wings! Why can't he wear tie and tails like everyone else? Mozart is not for an ill-mannered oaf in a business suit. To pick up his glass of water and look at it and turn it round and make a face as if there's poison in the glass – at the precise moment when the violinist begins to play? These are the tricks of a third-rate actor. A burlesque comic in a baggy suit. It turns a concert into a circus. It puts my blood in a rage. Don't they have any manners up there in Canada? I have to force myself to listen while he plays."

Ground beneath one's shoes - someone is searching - the-pursuit-of-things - announcing a great find - the wreck on the ocean floor - a dead-bolt drop to the depths - go on from there - fame that did him in - voices weave in and out - he takes a gold coin.

A biography, as I understand it, is an extended item of prose, purporting to contain all of the essential information about a person whose life one is asked to consider as one of importance.

An autobiography, as I would define it, is also an extended item of prose, one which purports to offer the same distillation of essence, but with the caveat – for those who are aware – that this 'exposé' has been concocted by the subject in question – one whose motives one might or might not be inclined to suspect.

One thing is for sure. I shall never, ever write my autobiography. Not in words, anyway – never in words.

> *"If rain fell upwards,*
> *it would wash the heavens,"*
> *said the first Village Wiseman.*

Recording the Goldberg Variations. Unlimited time and unlimited technology. The engineers do what I want and never complain.

Reporters scribbling notes as flashbulbs pop.

Playing it through and through again. Working my way inside the music. Listening to the play-backs of the various versions. Overruling the producer. Let's try it one more time. I'm reconsidering my approach. Twenty takes alone to get the opening theme. The publicity staff calls in the media. Could be on to something big. Playing up to the eager press. Posing at the piano. The photographers love the scarf and the gloves. Explaining the contents of my suitcase. Towels – spring-water – pills. How I soak my hands in hot water. My story about my dad's chair. Explaining my strange way of playing – all in the fingers and the mind. I've been jotting down phrases to use in the liner-notes. Thirty-eight minutes of music recorded in just a week.

There was a man who lived in Leipzig. He was simply known as Bach. His eyesight was failing; his health was poor. The other musicians looked askance at the music he wrote. He wrote the music it pleased himself to write.

Putting my name on a recording contract.
Recording for long hours in the studio.

"So what's all this talk about the North? Most Canadians live in cities – like Vancouver and Montreal. To them the North is cottage country – a hockey rink, a place to buy beer and a grocery store. The whole country huddles along their southern border. Afraid to put a foot on the Canadian Shield. All saving up so they can spend their retirement in Florida. Grumbling about having to go outside and shovel snow. Sure they talk with a funny accent, but Toronto is just a clean and polite New York. So I don't see what's so Canadian about the way he plays his music. And I don't see anything Canadian about Glenn Gould. It's all a gimmick – it's something different – it helps sell records. It's an image that's as subtle as a cartoon. I'm surprised he doesn't play piano in a Mounty uniform. Or walk on stage with an axe and a lumberjack shirt."

Experience as metaphor - from the moment of birth - appealing to be heard - all those on display - the music itself would tell me - the essence of the enterprise - creature who thrives on routine - simplified my life - in a neglected corner - imagining scores in my head.

Oh, of course I know what these people will do. They will thread a string of images from the surface of my life. They will present these images as the keys to the life of my mind.

Images like a little boy sitting at the key-board of a piano. Or of a faded program introducing the latest pianistic prodigy. Or of a muffled figure strolling beside a lake.

Or of fingers engaging a keyboard. Or of an earnest explicator inter-facing with a camera. A hand employing a hammer to open a clam.

"My dad says
don't look
at the sun."

Back home in Canada. At the cottage, at Lake Simcoe. Relaxing with the dog, under a tree.

Newspapers on a picnic table weighed down with a stone.

My Goldberg album propped up in the window of the cottage. Thirty versions of Glenn Gould on the cover. Reading the reviews in the New York newspapers. 'Skill and imagination' – 'sharp, clear technique' – 'intensity' – 'a young man with a future'. The trees sway back and forth in the breeze. The sunlight and the shadows on the reviews. 'Sensitive and superb' – 'clean-lined' – 'soberly expressive'. A motorboat drones in the distance. The water laps at the shore. Ecstatic praise for the new young pianist. Another cookie for the dog. The reviews are over the top. Exactly what I wanted them to be.

"Glenn Gould is making some of the most glorious music ever heard from a piano."

"There is no question that he will have the greatest career in the world."

The nectar
is still dripping
from the petals.

Newspaper stories about a new discovery.
Teenagers lining up with autograph books.
A boy playing a piano all alone.

The dew
is still moist
on the leaves.

Do you intend to write your own book someday?
An autobiography, or perhaps, a collaboration?
Could one of your personae write a biography of you?

You can go there
if you remember
where it is.

A best-seller in classical music. A resounding commercial success. Columbia has a new young star on its hands.

Eager fans waving pens and concert programs.

Standing on the world stage. Looking around and considering my prospects. In demand at twenty-three. Praised in Newsweek and the Saturday Review. Offers pouring in for appearances. Money funnelling into the bank-account. Carte blanche for any music I want to record. Offers from every province in Canada. Every state in the USA. Offers from England, France and Germany. Even an offer from Israel. The fastest-rising young star in the musical heavens. An invitation to come and play in the USSR.

Chapter 2

On stage at the Moscow Conservatory. A vast hall with many empty seats.

Rhythmic clapping from a crowd which fills a room.

The Canadian Embassy has offered free tickets. Perhaps many are here under duress. Determined that I shall make them all glad that they came. I play four fugues from the Art of the Fugue and the Partita No.6. I pretend, as much as I can, that I am alone. I concentrate on the music and ignore the concert hall. Forget the draught on my shoulders and the unfamiliar piano keys. I come back to hear a mighty roar of applause. Commotion outside as I rest at half-time and I am surprised to see the hall almost filled as I take my place again. Playing Bach, Beethoven and Berg. A Sweelinck fantasia – ten of the Goldberg Variations. A vast and appreciative audience – rhythmic clapping each time I stop. A basket of blue chrysanthemums is passed to the stage.

To measure one's own work and life

Concert patrons lining up around the block.
Bags in the trunk of an airport limousine.
Hands tying a present with a bow.

against

Do you often read the lives of famous people?
What do you look for when you read such a book?
Do you emphasize the childhood, the youth, the old age?

the rather staggering creative possibility.

A congregation singing an ancient hymn.
An audience of grim, worried faces.
Reporters scribbling in their notebooks.

Presenting a lecture-performance in Leningrad. Very similar to what I presented last week in Moscow. In the small hall of the Leningrad Conservatory. A presentation of works that are not played in the Soviet Union.

A fleet of missile-launchers in a May Day Parade.

A number of frowns as I make the announcement. Two of the professors stand up and make their way towards the door. Their effusive welcomes were translated when I arrived. Some of the students watch them uneasily. Even Bach has been thought to be too religious by some. Will the students all get up and leave? If they do, I will walk out myself. The Canadian Embassy staff looks grim – the Soviet Officials are carved in stone. The students hold ranks and I proceed with my offering to them. Berg's Sonata – Weburn's Variations. Some remarks and some examples from the Schoenberg school. They are very attentive listeners. I have no idea what they are thinking. Polite applause each time I pause. From the back, an occasional call for some Beethoven or some Bach. I enjoy the whole experience – the topic is a fresh and invigorating breeze, for me if not for Russia – but it is as if I am talking alone in an empty room. Are they free to express their thoughts or are they afraid? As a reward for their quiet patience, I do an encore of 'Best of Bach'. Thunderous ovations when I give them what they came to hear.

He was the subject of a musical mania. People packed the concert halls. Tickets sold for more than double. Aficionados passed the word. People lined up around the block in the dreary rain.

"Glenn Gould is a dedicated, sensitive poet of the keyboard."
"Glenn Gould is a pianist with rare gifts for the world."

I am looking down on nothing! I seem to be nothing myself! I am a being without form and void! I am nothing but a consciousness! Looking down on the spinning earth! It is nothing but rock and desert! Steam is rising from scraggly foliage! Cooling off from a heated state! I see no people anywhere! I see no animals or birds! But I see a glint of sunlight! I narrow my focus and I breathe a sigh of relief! Water is trickling down what looks like a cooling brook!

Theory of the future - afraid to put a foot - name your fee - what they came to hear - to seek inward - a single, first step - present my music from afar - guest who brings the fire - something grievously wrong.

My childhood simply doesn't matter. I really must insist that it doesn't. Of course, the best times were at the cottage – the best of all.

I had a piano in the cottage. A Chickering piano, built in 1895. I would play for hours on end.

Play the piano and go for walks with the dog. Bundle up nice and warm against the cold. Play the notes in my head as I walked along.

Every day Sisyphus rolled the rock.
Every night he lay down beside the hill.

Going out among the people. A Canadian in Russia. A little bout of sight-seeing before I go home.

A dignitary raising a glass and proposing a toast.

The traffic – the crowds – the buildings. As exotic to me as the moon. Meeting music-lovers and musicians. Small talk – speeches – meals. Jostling shoulders – hearty hugs – crushing handshakes. Tables piled with exotic foods. Pirozhki – slivki – borsch – ikra. Tea in steaming samovars. Turning down an endless round of vodka toasts. I ask the translator to please explain that I never indulge. They offer the best of themselves – they are hurt when I refuse. They reach out and I reach out, but music is the only point of contact. I am not like other people. I smile and they smile too, but the smiles are polite and confused. I wish I were back in my hotel room. I shall always dwell on the other side of the moon.

One day he packed his bags and caught the train. He proceeded up into the mountains for a three-week stay. To see his cousin and to savour the mountain air. One of the well visiting one of the not-so-well. Had he included an ample supply of his favourite cigar?

Flying across the Atlantic to perform in Europe.
Presenting Bach in Moscow and St. Petersburg.

I recognize the land and the water! Like a map on a table top! Two large lakes and a water-fall! What should be Toronto is mud and water! As if a flood has drained away! There are fledgling trees where my parents' house should be! Where the cottage should be, there is merely barren rock! Not a ship on the water and no sign of life on the shore! What should be Manhattan is just an island! Not a building or even a hut! Not one human seems to be here! Not a chipmunk or a deer! Two rivers flow past the island and out to the sea!

An actor clutching a wound - one tainted drop - impossible to know - the man was troubled - swallowed by a snake - keep their heads above water - he heard wonderful sounds - scanning the news - hoping for rain - a balancing act.

I learned to play the piano while sitting on my mother's knee. She was related to Edvard Grieg, the well-known Norwegian composer, though the spelling was not the same. She exposed me to music even before I was born.

She loved all those traditional old hymns. She would play them at church, on the organ – the music would swell and fill the space. As a result, I play the piano with organ-skills.

She used to teach me to sit up straight – feet flat on the floor. Told me I wasn't a virtuoso – not a Mozart-emerging-from-the-shell. In fact, the name of Mozart was banished from the family home.

At times, the fiddler stumbled.
At times, the fiddler fell.
The winds blew and the snow swirled all around him.
At times he guessed his way along the path.

Moving back and forth across Europe. Dashing through stations to catch the trains. Cold rooms – inedible food – draughty halls. *Driving rain pelting down on a train-station platform.*
Sitting in a railway compartment and reading a book. The scenery rushes by, but a book helps to make the time stand still. Too tired to study new scores. Performance drains one's sap away. My only stimulus when I'm tired is to read a book. Whatever seizes my mind. People send me books to read and I sometimes read those. Books about people who are living on mountains – books about painters who are trying to paint. Biographies of musicians – I must have read hundreds of those. I don't try to make myself think. I let what I'm reading sink right down to the bottom of my brain. The rain runs down the windowpane. I settle back in the seat. A perfect book for riding a train on a rainy day.

Haydn: Sonata No. 3 in E-flat major; Mozart: Sonata No. 10 in C major, K.330; Fantasia and Fugue in C major, K.394 / Haydn: Piano Sonata No. 59 / Mozart: Piano Sonata No. 10 / Mozart: Fantasia and Fugue / Beethoven: Concerto No. 1 in C major; Bach: Concerto No. 5 in F minor / Bach: Keyboard concerto No. 5 / Beethoven: Piano Concerto No. 1 / Berg: Sonata for Piano, Op. 1; Schoenberg: Three Piano Pieces, Op. 11; Krenek: Sonata No. 3 for Piano, Op. 92, No. 4 / Berg: Piano Sonata, Op. 1 / Schoenberg: Three Piano Pieces, Op. 11 / Krenek: Piano Sonata No. 3, Op. 92, No. 4 / Gould: String Quartet No. 1 / String Quartet in F minor, Op. 1 /

The public concert, as we know it today, will wither and disappear. New technology will cause it to fade away. It surprises me that my theory is controversial. Some are predicting the birth of an atomic-age monster. Why debate whether the sun should come up at dawn?

Headlines touting the praises of a native son.
A man sleeping beside an enormous rock.
A person lost on a mountain in a snowstorm.

That sort of categorizing \ the vertical and horizontal dimensions \ the values that we attach to art \ similar but not identical \ become his own com-

poser \ this recurring dream \ emphasize every possible connection \ to mingle perspectives \ interprets by its own lights \ realize the true intentions.

Do you often spend time thinking of your childhood?
Are there moments in childhood that made you what you are?
Could you pick one day or one moment when everything changed?

His parents had a cottage by a lake.

Hot tea steaming in a samovar.
A land with no animals or people.
The sun shining down on a tennis court.

"Glenn is a natural-born showman – leads the media by the nose. He often chuckles and refers to himself as a ham. Reporters love it when he teases them – saying the suitcase full of pills is just a valise. This whole health thing is a publicity bonanza – 'The Hypochondriac Classical Pianist.' Glenn has the media dancing on a string."

A triumphal return to Canada. A big splash in all the Toronto newspapers. Local boy makes good and all of that.
A choice of newspapers on a rack in a coffee shop.
I slip away to the cottage. Keep the interviews to a minimum. The only thing I want, from now on, is time. Everybody insists on reading me the reviews. 'An epoch-making series of concerts.' – 'Glenn Gould is a golden boy.' – 'Beyond human comprehension.' – 'Something high above the earth.' You conquered Moscow, Glenn – something Napoleon couldn't do. You've got everybody talking at the samovar. And Toronto – stuffy Toronto – Toronto never praises its own. Well you forced them to make an exception in your case. 'Cheers upon cheers.' – 'Encores upon encores.' – 'Our native son has done his native country proud.' You got them eating out of your hand, Glenn. To them you can do no wrong – like a hockey player who scores an overtime goal. Who says that a prophet doesn't get a fair shake at home?

The countryside was much more tranquil than the city. From time to time the painter would paint or make a sketch. But he felt that there was always a missing element. Why paint or make a sketch when there is always something missing? The missing element that would be sure to make it art.

"Glenn Gould plays these pieces like a nasty little boy trying to put one over on his piano teacher."
"Glenn Gould's latest disk is the most loathsome recording of Mozart ever made."

I am closer now to the ground! I can no longer see the curve of the earth! High cliffs and the sky above! A beach with a ribbon of sand! Lapping waves where the land and the water meet! I am six feet above the ground! I look down and make a decision! I stamp what might be my foot with a thud! I raise it up and look beneath! I am relieved to see a footprint on the sand!

Looks at it through borrowed eyes - absorbed all of life - a person talking earnestly - probe the nightmares - a handful of primeval slime - that was impossible - the matching of place and self - voices are each distinct - a foolish thing to do - roles are going to change.

I used to drive the car to the lake when I was only about six years old. I would steer the car while sitting on my father's knee. He built a chair for me which I still use to this day.

I still love to drive cars. I close the windows tight and lock all the doors. I turn the radio on – to whatever the airwaves bring.

I drive for miles and miles nearly every day. I go further North now than I ever did before. Take a room and work on a project for weeks at a time.

"Make any wish you might like,"
said the magician
to the archer.

A moment's peace at the cottage. A chance to re-pack my bags before heading out on my North American tour.
A lawn, two leisure chairs and lapping waves.
My manager sits down beside me. Hey Glenn, I just got off the phone. Music is starving for people like you. You bring people into the concert halls who don't know classical music from the squawking of the passing streetcar wheels. You're building up quite a following. Girls with your picture on their bedroom walls. Like a movie star or a soap star on TV. The money is rolling in like the tide on the Coney Island beach. In demand at every venue. Name any amount you want and they'll think they're getting a bargain. Stick a pin anywhere on the map and name your fee.

Bach was valued as a cobbler or a tailor. His living conditions were dismal and dark. An operation on his eyesight had failed. He was nearly paralyzed. He continued writing the music that everyone shunned.

Spending much of my time in railway stations.
Grateful to have a brief moment to read a book.

A phone call to a friend.
"So what do you think of this, as a tentative scenario? People are sit-

ting in a movie theatre. Let's say it's a Saturday afternoon. Winter, perhaps, so there's not much to do outside. And it's one of those corny old-fashioned movies. The new movies don't come to the small towns. When the city gets tired of a movie, they pass it on. Anyway, it's a movie about a spaceship which is landing in a small town. It's sitting and throbbing in a farmer's field. Way out past the high school football field. And everybody crowds around it – trampling the stubble on the ground – keeping a distance so they can run. And then a door opens in the side of this celestial contrivance. Now this is the interesting thing: not only does a ramp come down in the field where the spaceship lands, but it extends right into the theater where the people are watching. And these people stand up right away – jump right out of those theatre seats – and many back away and some just stand. But one young boy – the theatre usher – moves forward, and puts his foot on this glowing ramp. 'Greetings from Earth!' the boy calls out. 'If I understand you truly, you wish an Earthling to return with you to your planet! Let me be the one to do so! I would welcome a friendly exchange! I shall enter your celestial contrivance, but on one condition only – that you will allow me to return whenever I please!' "

A standard of perfection - the psychobiographical process - alone among the many - water assuming form - the little bird went soaring - people magazine - on a turntable, turning round - what a waste - i am not a pilot - all the promise.

It was my parents who owned the cottage. Used to take me there whenever they could spare the time. The Philharmonic on the radio with everything covered in snow.

People laugh when I say that Lake Simcoe is in the North. I just smile and say, "Well, it's the North until you get there, and then you find that the North is further North." All the music I like is Northern music to me.

It was my parents who recognized the talent in me. My mother is gone now and I don't see my father too often anymore. I went out to the car and talked with him when he brought me a present last Christmas Eve.

The little bird
was perched
on the edge of the nest.

A full day working up a new score. Europe seems a million miles away.
A visiting celebrity posing beside a kangaroo.
The offers are pouring in for future tours. Hawaii – China – Japan. So many places I would like, someday, to see. The Australians are very persistent. They have been courting me ever since the Goldberg came out. I have heard that they work their visiting artists to death. My manager assures me that they will listen to reason. The terms are a very good financial remuneration. If we

can eliminate the exhaustion quotient, you'll find that it won't be so bad. I'm sure they'll listen to reason to get you to come. The sun is setting over the trees. The water is lapping at the dock. Easy to forget what touring is like at the end of such days.

"Glenn Gould displays a profound technical, intellectual and emotional identification with the music."

"It is inconceivable that somewhere in the world one might hear a greater performance than has been presented by Glenn Gould this afternoon."

The sun
still rises
in the morning.

Moviegoers eating popcorn in a movie-show.
A crowd engaged in rhythmic clapping.
A single human footprint in the sand.

The sun still
pauses
at noon.

What was it like when you spent summers at the cottage?
What was it like to walk in the woods?
Do you yearn for those days when it was just you and your dog?

The sun
still sets
at the end of the day.

Looking over a grand estate. My manager at my elbow. An estate-agent showing me around.
A celebrity foursome teeing off for a round of golf.
Only fifteen miles from Toronto. Views of the river from the balcony. Seven bathrooms – a breakfast room – a scullery. A swimming pool and a tennis court. A whole wing which would be perfect for a recording studio. Here you could make an office for a personal manager. The piano could overlook the swimming pool. Social evenings at the golf club, a bridle path and country walks. Easy access to the airport – limousine service around the clock. Facts and figures swarm like hornets as the estate-agent gives his spiel. His voice echoes as he talks in the empty room. A little day-dream and then I snap back. The only thing I say is – I know that Van Cliburn has bought an estate, but it's not for me. I must have been thinking of a movie of my career.

Chapter 3

Shuttling back and forth between Europe and North America. One tour joined to another, like coupled cars on the high-speed trains. A schedule in my pocket with the dates and the towns. Uneasy, and I know exactly why.

Taxis throbbing in a mid-town traffic snarl.

I am not a recording artist. I am not a recording artist at all. I am a travelling concert-pianist, a peripatetic vaudevillian, who takes a moment here and there to cut a record. Always in a hurry – always a man with a plane or a train to catch. A date to play the same pieces of music that I have played so often before. No time to listen to the play-back. No time to re-record. No time to remove the offending note – the flaw that makes me unhappy with every recording I do.

To seek inward

A crowd lining up at an airport.
A row of adjudicators testing a little boy.
A phone ringing in the middle of the night.

for the shape

Would you say that you have had a damaged youth?
Lonely, rebellious, angry, misunderstood?
Isn't that what every artist is bound to say?

of one's life.

A technician plugging in a row of heaters.
A patient in a clinic waiting-room.
A clutch of bubbles dancing on a breeze.

Flying back to Europe. The Salzburg Festival. A week of restless dreams about flying on a plane.

A burning aeroplane hurtling towards the ground.

Sick to my stomach in Salzburg. Cancelling because of a sudden attack of the flu. Flying to London to make some recordings for the BBC. Bach – Haydn – Hindemith. Sweelinck – Krenek – Berg. Flying back again to Salzburg. Two recitals and off to Lucerne. Bach's D-minor concerto. High fever and perspiration. Having to constantly wipe my eyes. I go out on stage and bow and start to play. Surprisingly, my performance has very few flaws. I am surprised when I receive a standing ovation, but no applause is worth the agony that I am forcing myself to go through. I am a baggy-pants vaudevillian – a pork-pie hat and a big red nose. I cancel my last performance and fly back home. The drone of the engines keeps me awake. I don't ever want to fly to Europe again.

He became a musical phenomenon. Heaps of praise in every review. The music world had found its standard-bearer. The great tradition was safe for now. He could reproduce the music as it had always been heard.

"Glenn Gould flings himself into these pieces with evident glee."
"It is impossible not to be infected with Glenn Gould's joy."

"If Glenn takes to you, he'll put your phone number on his list. The first phone call from Glenn will be the most exhilarating and intimidating phone call of your life. Now, you're on the list! You're on the list as one of the recipients of those magnificent verbal performances. Those idea-soliloquies that run to hours on the phone – in the middle of the night for you, but not for Glenn – which give you glimpses into the mind of a genius at work. The mind which takes Mozart and Beethoven apart – nut by nut and bolt by bolt. But people sometimes misunderstand when Glenn phones them up and plays a newly-recorded piece of music. They sometimes think that he wants to hear their opinion. He doesn't. Glenn is not one of those insecure artists who is desperate for praise. Not one of those shallow novices who is wondering whether his work is good or not. No – Glenn is offering the purest thing that a friend can give. He wishes to share something which has given him exquisite pleasure. The purest gift is that which requires no equivalent response. He asks absolutely nothing in return. Glenn offers music for which there need be no applause."

This kid from canada - in embryonic form - thread a string of images - continued writing the music - a musical mania - a clutch of bubbles - wearing a paper mask - that force that cracks the jar - in full flight - detected a tiny flaw.

Of course, I had a piano teacher – I've never denied it. Every child prodigy should have one. I've heard that his feelings were hurt because I didn't acknowledge his crimes.

We fought like cats and dogs. Snarling and hissing for hours each day. He was the cat and I – as you might guess – emerged as the dog.

What I learned from my piano teacher is that talent is the one thing that you simply cannot teach. Talent and originality are the two unteachables. Everything else can be taught in half an hour.

> *A man*
> *painted bars*
> *on his face.*

A room in a hotel. The Hotel Vier Jahreszeiten in Hamburg. Cancelling nine performances.

A cleaning lady listening to music through an open door.

Suffering from the flu. 101 degrees. Chronic bronchitis in the right lung. No hope of a speedy recovery. Tempted to cancel the rest of the tour. I can't be expected to play when I am ill. In bed for ten days with almost nothing to eat. Rice porridge and fruit salad day after day. X-rays and other tests. 'Focal nephritis' is a frightening term. My manager sends a telegram. 'Urging you to get back on your feet.' He has never played a note in a concert hall. The doctor expresses concern about my kidneys. Writing a cheque to Wolfgang Kollisch, the impresario, for his losses. Money well spent in return for my time. All of the friends who express their concerns are thousands of miles away. The greatest blessing in all of this is that I am alone.

Mountain vistas on every side. One of the well among those who were ill. Life and death in a store-front window and he outside. Then a catarrh and a nose dripping blood. Can anyone stay well in the land of the ill?

Flying back and forth across the ocean.
Spending my happiest moments alone in hotel rooms.

"Glenn is what you could call a totally original voice. Most people in an era will think along the same lines. Politicians, social activists – artists as well. And there are no people who are more herd-like than musicians. Everybody in the herd is moving in the same direction. They may disagree on what particular path to take, but not one of them questions the direction of the herd. Buffalo, elk, cattle – even lemmings – are all the same. Musical thought is leveled down. Original thinkers – rare as they are – are taken in and made orthodox by the herd. Glenn is always rejecting this tendency. Glenn is always moving in a direction of his own."

Ready for the day ahead - make a trajectory - measure that trait - a needle riding smoothly - sliding past the poisoned fangs - scratch a curve with a stick - gradually emerging with a profile - any peace of mind - centres of balance - feeling the limits.

When I was eleven, I began to enter competitions. The competitions were a disservice to humanity. The highest bidder was given a ticket to mediocrity.

Every moderator was a former child-prodigy. Every piece had been played the same way a thousand times. Every competitor was a surrogate for a curdled adult dream.

I always saw a competition as a bullfight. A suit of lights and a two-edged sword. You were the matador and the bull who you were so intent on dispatching in the blood-stained dust turned out to be you.

Does the dog
know who I am?,
the man wondered.

I have come to the end of the line. I sit here in a rental car a long, long way from the cottage at Uptergrove. I stare out onto acres of shifting sand.

A piano in the shimmering sunlight of a desert mirage.

It is not Israel – it is me. It is me who is just not ready for Israel. A leaden piano whose joyous notes sound more like funeral bells. Another piano which seems to have hands which reach out and clutch mine, so I have to wrestle, like Jacob, for every note. A hall converted from a shed down at the dockside. Cold air whistling past the sacks that seal the doors. A bank of heaters humming on stage – an obbligato to the pieces that I play. I am a camel who has run out of water – crossing a desert without a well. I ask myself if this is what I was born to do. What to do? – What to do? I put my rental car in gear, clear the sand with the windshield wipers, and drive away.

Beethoven: Piano Concerto No. 3 in C minor, Op. 37 / Piano Concerto No. 3 / Bach: Italian Concerto in F major & Partita Nos. 1 & 2 / Italian Concerto, BWV 971 / Partita No. 1 in B-flat major, BWV 825 / Partita No. 2 in C minor, BWV 826 / Brahms: 10 Intermezzi / Intermezzo in A major, Op. 76, No. 6 / Intermezzo in A minor, Op. 76, No. 7 / Intermezzo in E major, Op. 116, No. 4 / Intermezzo in E-flat major, Op. 117, No. 1 / Intermezzo in B-flat minor, Op. 117, No. 2 / Intermezzo in C-sharp minor, Op. 117, No. 3 / Intermezzo in A minor, Op. 118, No. 1 / Intermezzo in A major, Op. 118, No. 2 / Intermezzo in E-flat minor, Op. 118, No. 6 / Intermezzo in B minor, Op. 119, No. 1 /

The impresario has a building. Heat and hydro – taxes and bills. He has an audience whom he has groomed. That audience makes demands which he, in turn, must obey. The zoo-keeper trembles when he hears the lions roar.

A painter unsure of what to paint.

A person speaking into a microphone.
A magician pulling a rabbit out of a hat.

A convincing rationale \ hold together structurally \ the precise ana-
lytical concepts \ problem of narration \ the whole subsurface \ a new kind of
listener \ an improvisatory freedom \ control the flow of information \ a pas-
sacaglia of fact \ supportive elements of the texture.

Did you have any rapport with anyone in your high school?
Did you and any teenage musicians get along?
Would you say that you were a youth without any friends?

The boy was born with a wonderful ear for music.

A row of fresh-baked cookies on a tray.
The loud drone of an aeroplane.
A person in a jar with a lid on top.

"His ears – his eyes – his throat. His sense of balance – pains in his
chest. Inability to sleep – a runaway pulse. Glenn mentions these symptoms all
the time, but how can anyone assess the health of a hypochondriac?"

Here I am, at the top of the pile. The bijoux in the window which the
spotlight most admires. The envy of every triangle-player in the world.
A prisoner with diamond manacles binding his hands.
So what exactly does the spotlight reveal? Maestro Bernstein coming
to me with his friendly request, as I limber up my hands in the green-room
sink. Maestro Szell entertaining the orchestra – hearty laughs all round – as I
supervise the adjustments to my chair. Mr. Hupfer insisting that he knows the
Horowitz sound. Records spinning on turntables with errors clogging their
grooves. Pianos that bark, pianos that growl, pianos that bare their teeth and
bite. Reviewers who dip their pens in the blood of their latest kill.

Should art be of the East or of the West? Western art is all about people. Eastern art is all about things. The 'Praying Spirits' of Iwasa Metabei? Or
the 'Ophelia' of Millais?

"Glenn Gould is a musical parasite – thumbing down greatness and
hitching on for a ride."
"If Beethoven flinches his shoulder – Glenn Gould will fall off on the
pavement and crawl off to lie in a ditch by the side of the road."

"Oh – Glenn Gould! Glenn Gould! Glenn Gould! I get sick of hearing the name! An adolescent show-off. A bully in the playground. The kid

who splashes water in your face. He has desecrated piece after piece of the classical-music heritage. His shtick is very simple – a beginner's parlour-trick. Playing every piece at a different tempo. If it's slow – play it faster; if it's fast – play it slow. How could such a simple tactic shake up the music world? And his disrespect for the giants – well it's all been done before. Climbing up on the shoulder of a great one and shouting that you're taller than he. Bernard Shaw assaulting Shakespeare with sticks and stones. The loudest mouth commands the most ears. I'll leave you with just one question: what has Glenn Gould ever written that is equal – not to the best – but to what would have amounted to an off-day for Mozart or Beethoven? What has he ever composed that is equal to the least of Bach?"

The last guest to arrive - the amateur-king - move on past it - a complete review of the events - an ideal relationship - major failure in life - such debilitating symptoms - harder for glenn to find - the unseen person in the group - an exploration of an idea.

You had to submit to the cookie-cutter before you could play. You couldn't smile, you couldn't breathe, you couldn't grow. You couldn't brush your dog's hair from your suit as you played.

You were trapped underneath the piano, with its weight upon your chest. Someone else's music, played for someone else, by someone who wasn't me. I won every contest I entered as a boy.

I chewed up students twice my age and spit them out. I absorbed them into my bloodstream, like a ghoul – a glenn-ghoul. They were all trying to be what I came to be.

A boy
carved his name
in the bark of a tree.

Taking stock of my career so far. It is clear to me that working with people has never been my forté. I do not wish to compete for the votes of the crowd.

A celebrity cast in wax and left out in the sun.

I am weary of the system. I was weary when I was a boy. The system distorts emerging careers. Impresarios keep their charges in an impresarios' convenient jar. Maestros keep their protégées in a maestro's convenient jar. Reviewers keep performers in a reviewer's convenient jar. Patrons keep virtuosos in a patron's convenient jar. They don't pound you into a jelly – as one would a combative foe. They invite you to liquefy yourself – to make yourself into a compliant, malleable entity. Then you pour yourself into a jar and the lid is closed. I would like to present my music from afar. The rays of the sun are always welcome, but the sun is ninety-three million miles from the earth. I am

Glenn Gould – that force that cannot be contained. I am Glenn Gould – that force that cracks the jar.

There was a Count who had everything that anyone could want. He ate from golden plate. Ornate rings adorned his hands. His castle clung to a mountain with an endless view. Only one thing in the world was not his to command.

Cancelling a number of concerts due to illness.
Yearning for the day when I can go home.

"So elusive is Glenn Gould that he can advance an idea, turn it around and around in a discussion of its implications, and then withdraw himself, so that all you have is the idea, with no knowledge of Glenn Gould's personal opinion on the topic. You are left with a lot of idea and very little Glenn Gould. 'The redirection of ambition-patterns.' – 'The reaffirmation of traumatic associations.' These are terms he will use as a fog. He picks them out of the air. Dark labels on a door. Such phrases are graffiti on a brick wall which protects Glenn Gould from the intimate gaze of nosy neighbours. And as for Glenn Gould's dreams – I have never been sure that they are his dreams. Why does he tell them and then break off when you try to respond? I've suspected for years and years that he makes them up. He's like a little boy who is wearing a paper mask. There's no limit to the mystery of the Glenn Gould mind."

Children clambered on - inspired interior monologue - an individual in a crowd - a jar assuming form - translating classical music - rumour has it - the paint had washed away - a truly inferior musician - you have poisoned the pilot - just me alone.

I was only actually myself when I was at the cottage. Long walks with the dog around the lake or in the woods. At the cottage all the music was inside my head.

So why enter these competitions?, you might well ask. Why indeed? Why indeed?

Let's both of us think of a person who climbs a mountain. Now the climbing of a mountain always begins with a single, first step. Does he intend to dwell one step above the ground?

"Whose recording
do you think God was listening to
as he was creating the universe?"

Reading a book that was sent to me by an admirer.
A person made of ink distilled from a book.

Life as a series of bubbles. Bubbles of sunshine – bubbles of rain. The girl O-Nami: – her outer-surface – her inner pain. The embryo-artist: – to be a Metabi? – to be a Millais? An hour of living inside this novel. Is it possible to shape one's life as a haiku? To live one's life as a water-droplet – connected or not-connected to the world? Such questions are the bridge-slats over the abysses of countless canyons. A coincidence that I am reading this book on a train.

"Glenn Gould has created an atmosphere that is just mesmerizing."
"One is electrified by the power, the authority, the sustained tension by which Glenn Gould compels one's fascinated attention."

When did
the note
most clearly sound?

A spokesperson delivering the final word.
A cleaning lady squinting at the words on a record-sleeve.
A piano teacher tapping out the time.

Did you
taste feel smell
hear and see?

Any contact now with any particular person from your teenage years?
Any person from that time you sometimes phone?
Any person from that time you might like to see?

Did you seal it
in a locket
or set it free?

The University of Toronto. Invited to give the Convocation address. An honourary degree as a Doctor of Law.
A bearded sage dispensing wisdom in the agora.
Hundreds of caps and gowns. I lean in to the microphone. What do I say to them? Well, I will certainly say what I often say to myself. It is important to convince oneself of the futility of living too much by the advice of others. The only advice that one should heed is that of oneself. Afterwards I am interviewed by a reporter. I intend, soon, to give up concert work. I have a few more obligations and then I'll be free. The reporter chuckles as he writes my comments down. You've made this claim before, Mr. Gould. More than once, as I recall. What do you say to people who don't believe it's true?

Chapter 4

I have decided that I will never go back to play in Europe – never again.
A man making notes as he rides in a train.

I will concentrate on North America. I will stay as close as I can to home. I will concentrate on the things that I most enjoy to do – studying scores and building interpretations and recording them and then moving on to the next and the next and the next. I will write essays explaining my theories. How does the composer relate to the musician relate to the auditor-in-chief? Who has the most important role in this chain of command? I have a life-time of exploration and explanation still to live. From now on, concerts will only serve to pay the bills.

To make

A boy drinking water beside a well.
A patient standing in front of an x-ray machine.
A maestro tapping urgently with his baton.

thirty interesting pieces

What was your relationship with your teachers?
Do you value what they did for you?
What would you say was the biggest gain of your student years?

into one.

A painter with his paint-box under his arm.
A glass of water and a little pile of pills.
Magazines for sale at a newsstand.

And I will never fly in a plane – ever again. I will take the train or drive to wherever I have to be. I can take the train to New York whenever I am to record. I can leave enough time in my schedule to take the train anywhere in North America where I am scheduled to perform. Flying all these years has taken a relentless toll.

A hand holding a torch at arm's length.

I want to record all of the corpus which I admire. I want to write articles in which I explain my approach. I want to develop recording techniques which will break the bonds of the concert hall. I want to be free to follow the paths of my ideas. Above all, I want to compose. I want to compose whatever music I am capable of writing. I want to write at the highest level which I can attain. What a cold world this would be without the music. The composer is the guest who brings the fire.

He was the new and he was the old. The heir of Chopin, Clementi, Hummel, Liszt and John Field. The same concert repertoire in the same performances as they. A conduit for the music, from the composer straight to the ear. But young enough to brush the dust off the concert halls.

"Glenn Gould is in full flight and in full command of his creative powers."

"Listening to Glenn Gould play the piano has something of the intensity of a religious revelation."

I am dancing on a stage! It is the stage at Stratford, Ontario! I am enjoying myself immensely! It is the music of Tchaikovsky! I am flowing as if I am liquid! I am the music and the music is me! Every move is a fluid expression of my deepest self! But something is not quite right! I sense the presence of other dancers! I begin to wonder whether I am alone on stage!

Ours to enjoy - the surface of my life - this celestial contrivance- dedicated, sensitive poet - a cleaning lady listening - no limit to the mystery - one thing in the world - in full command - the music stops.

I spent two years at my parents' cottage. After I left the Conservatory. I felt that my teachers had exhausted their repertoire.

Just a need to get away. A need to leave the city behind with all its noise and busy confusion. A need to concentrate on the making of the self.

Of course North is a state of mind with we Canadians. Any place where you are standing is the spot where North begins. Any movement North is a cleansing of the mind.

He watched as the old fellow watched.
Surging horses, a unicorn, laughing children.
The children for the next ride stood in line.

The bass entrance was wrong, and I knew that it was wrong. Bar twenty-five in Book One. But I had to catch this train so I couldn't stay.

A man hailing a taxi in a traffic-jam.

I know how recordings can be made. I know how they will be made – with the technology which we have – with the technology which we will demand – with the technology which we will devise. The listener is trapped in time, in the chaos of the moment – the squeal of the tires outside his apartment, the sound of the streetcar and the people next door – but the music should come to the listener as from a cloud. It should be as perfect as this world is able to provide. It should be flawless because the maker took it seriously – because the maker took the time to make it perfect – because the maker is as serious about the music as the listener is serious about himself.

He wondered of what the human being consists. Ectoplasm, endo-plasm, blood? Memory, compassion, thought? He saw his own skeleton in an x-ray machine. Was there any sort of life beyond the grave?

Restricting my travel-range to North America.
Studying the new advances in technology.

I am not alone on stage! I am dancing in a chorus! I seem to be wear-ing a costume! A costume with feathers and glue! It is the chorus of Swan Lake! My every move is the move of everyone else on the stage! Suddenly, there is a shout! "No! No! No! There is something grievously wrong! I have detected a tiny flaw in the presentation!" The music stops, the dancers stop and the audience starts to buzz! I stop dancing as well and the lights are harsh on my eyes!

Explains the richter scale - tending the sacred flame - isn't there as himself - glenn gould's response - lifted itself off the ground - born into time - a sense of the shape - right next to divine - waves of sound - a foreign element.

No, I was never in favour of leading the concert life. That was never an ideal occupation for me. I could see far past the limits of others' goals.

But I needed an entré, you see. Something to open up the doors. I knew that A would lead to B and far beyond.

I settled on the Goldberg. To make it everything that was me. I would be Bach and the Count and Goldberg all in one.

*The peasants were
starving outside the walls.*

Reading biographies of all the great composers. Writing essays on the composers whom I know. What is there in the life that illuminates the music? What is there in the music that illuminates the life?

A clean, white, empty sheet of paper.

Richard Strauss is sitting at a café. All the weight of his father on his back. He has just had a talk with Alexander Ritter. Outside the window, across the street, Ritter waits for the streetcar to stop. He climbs aboard and he is on his way. Time goes by – the coffee grows cold – it was bitter anyway. Pencil and paper on the table. Strauss draws the needed lines. He leans forward and begins to fill the page.

Beethoven: Piano Concerto No. 4 in G major, Op. 58 / Piano Concerto No. 4 / Mozart: Piano Concerto No. 24 in C minor, K. 491 & Schoenberg: Piano Concerto, Op. 42 / Mozart: Piano Concerto No. 24 / Schoenberg: Piano Concerto / Bach: The Art of the Fugue, Volume I / The Art of Fugue, Fugues 1 – 9 / Strauss: Enoch Arden (Tennyson), Op. 38 / Enoch Arden / Bach: The Well-Tempered Clavier, Book I Volume I, BWV 846-853 / The Well-Tempered Clavier, Book I, Preludes and Fugues 1 – 8 / Bach: Partitas 3 & 4, Toccata 7 / Partita No. 3 in A minor, BWV 827 / Partita No. 4 in D major, BWV 828 / Toccata No. 7 in E minor /

The Maestro as star performer. Brilliant smile and flowing hair. He must keep the patrons coming back for more. Applause for the ever-narrowing range of his repertoire. He well knows by whom the baton is being waved.

Crumpled paper in a wastebasket beside a piano.
A flock of dancers flowing across a stage.
A man who seeks a recipe for sleep.

Seem to belong organically \ a seriousness of intent \ multiple-authorship responsibility \ metaphorical illusions \ the listener-consumer participant \ to perfect a structure \ interrelate his vertical and horizontal intentions \ independent and hermit-like \ psychologically naive and architecturally destructive.

Was there an inevitable antagonism with your teachers?
Did some of them bring out the worst in you?
Were you competing with your teachers when you were a child?

He could play the piano better than anyone else.

Peasants lining up with begging bowls.
A conductor punching tickets on a train.
A choreographer laying down the law.

"Glenn has a very unhealthy lifestyle. A pill or two for every ache and pain. They say that a person who is his own lawyer is a fool; well, both the patient and the doctor are Glenn himself."

Does a musician take time off to write the music? Does the music buoy him up as he walks the street? Does he weave himself into every composition? A drop of blood for every single note?

A sliver of morning sunlight on a cold, bare floor.

Arnold Schoenberg opens his eyes. Morning? Of course it is, though there is barely enough light for him to see. The room is cold and dark. Last night the candle worked its way down to a stub. Take the poker and stir the ashes of the coals. The tiny glow lights the man wiping his eyes. The sun's first rays show the piano dwarfing the room. Who will want to listen to this music? Who will appreciate this music if it is heard? He brushes these thoughts away like cobwebs in a museum. He splashes some water into the bowl. A cold shock on his hands and his face. Then he sits down at the piano once again.

How to keep thought in its proper place? To make art which is nothing but thought? To make art out of no thought at all? All these thoughts moved the painter's mind and idled his hand. He thought as the sun went up and the sun went down.

"Glenn Gould should just play all the most popular pieces in the way that people want them to be played."

"What people want is the Classical Music Hit Parade."

A man is approaching the stage! He is coming out of the audience! There are whispers in the crowd! "It is Mr. Ivanov! Lev Ivanovich Ivanov! The great choreographer!" "Who is that boy in the chorus! The one far at the back! You there! Stand still! Your footwork is atrocious! Let us have that note again!" The piano player plays the same note three times! Mr. Ivanov bends down and moves my right foot an inch to the left! "This is where your right foot should be when that note is being played! You must learn to respect the work! You must serve the dance!"

A very harsh world - an interesting study - didn't want to go there - i have a vision - see very deeply inside - major area of concern - threatened my whole career - eggs throbbing at night - representatives of ideas - the warmth and the cold.

Yes, I practised at the piano. Many hours of many days. But I have always felt that the music takes place in the mind.

So – long walks with the dog by the lakeshore. Long walks with the dog in the woods. Take the boat out and go for miles with the notes in my head.

I was always making progress. Always making something new. Every note took its place in the larger musical web.

> *"If it did, the earth*
> *would be completely dry,"*
> *said the second Village Wiseman.*

Reading about myself as portrayed in newspapers and magazines. Time – Life – Look. Newsweek – The New Yorker – Saturday Review. I have a service which sends me every one.

A handsome young man on the cover of a magazine.

'Exotic, unique, eccentric.' 'Unpredictable, elusive, self-contained.' 'He wears gloves in warm weather.' 'He wears a coat in the August heat.' 'He hums out loud when he is playing.' 'He brings a glass of water on stage.' 'He travels with a suitcase full of pills.' 'He is afraid to fly in airplanes.' 'He never plays a piece as it has been played.' 'He believes that he knows Mozart better than Mozart.' 'He believes that he knows Beethoven better than Beethoven.' 'He looks down on these greats from a very high hill.' 'Some day he might come to know Glenn Gould.' I take them along with me and read them on the trains. Glenn Gould reading a magazine which purports to provide the low-down on the real Glenn Gould.

The Count was weighted with care. Matters domestic and matters foreign. Always a crisis – never peace. The Count was no longer able to sleep. The Court Musician had exhausted his repertoire.

Planning a life of study and thought and recording.
Yearning for the day when I will be free.

A phone call to a friend.

"Let's say there's a shepherd boy, back in Biblical times. Or it could be anywhere primitive, even today. And he is looking after his sheep, and he takes a drink of water, and he realizes that his flask – a goatskin with a stopper in it, I suppose, slung on a string of leather around his neck – is just about dry. So he drives his sheep – perhaps fifteen or so, adult, and some lambs, if this is the spring – over to another field where there is a well. And he drops the bucket down – made of wood with metal bands – and draws up a nice cool soothing draught of spring-fed water. But as he lets it flow over his chin and down his tunic – the day is hot, I assume – he leans back a bit too far and falls into the well. Now what is he going to do? He can hear his sheep bleating. They wonder where he's gone. And the boy spends many hours in the well. Standing in water up to his knees. But then he finally hears some voices. Must be the other shepherds – his father and his uncle and the other men. So he sings the Song of Danger – taught by his mother when he was a boy. His voice acquires an echo from the well. The men all crowd around – blocking out the light – and look down at him. 'Please get me out of here!' he cries. 'I fell down into the well and cannot get out!' Again the sound reverberates. 'Stay down there!' his father shouts. His voice, too, has an echo. 'But I will die if I stay here!' the boy shouts back. 'A reasonable price to pay!' the father shouts, in return. 'All the men and I agree! Your singing is to die for! You sing the Danger Song as no one else! We have never heard a voice with a keener sound!' "

Every child was on a unicorn - reduced to its skeleton - guarded and obscure - completely in harmony - a perfect note - wants an anecdote - the mental imagery - a truly important musician - what does it all mean - this is my choice.

For two years I lived in the cottage. Hardly saw anyone from outside. Just myself and the dog and the music and very little else.

But I could see New York from there. I could see the nut I would crack. The eggs in the wicker basket left under the tree.

After two years I was ready. Ready for Washington and New York. A fresh breeze from way up in the North was coming to town.

"Why would
your dad
say that?"

Certainly publicity is a very important ingredient of the creative process. If people have never heard of one's work, they cannot buy it and they cannot appreciate it. So I am a cheerful co-operator in the publicity game.

Flashbulbs lighting a room like fireworks.

In fact, I rather enjoyed the process in the early days. 'The young genius, Glenn Gould, at the piano, in overcoat and gloves.' 'The Canadian Iceman thawing out as he gets ready to play.' But after a certain amount of repetition, I began to get a little irritated with requests to repeat such poses again and again. The media kept tossing me flowers, but I got tired of catching the same old faded bouquet. All the imaginative-renewal had to come from inside. Catch me unawares in hat and gloves in a draughty concert hall, and you have the real Glenn Gould. If it helps to gain attention – all to the good. But ask me to pose in the same hat and gloves – Glenn Gould as an actor playing a Mme.-Tussaud-Glenn-Gould – and the career takes on the veneer of Hollywood.

"Few pianists match Glenn Gould in the discipline, sharp focus and scrupulous artistry he brings to the playing of Bach."

"Glenn Gould plays in compelling style, with a rhythmic flexibility that maintains the tension in each complex work."

The daisies
in the meadow

are in full bloom.

Two people talking heatedly in a café.
A person strolling beside a calm lake.
A young child astride a unicorn.

Do we pick them
or do we leave them
to dance in the breeze?

Did you know yourself as a musician from your earliest years?
Would you say that you have largely taught yourself?
That you are one of those rare artists who is self-propelled?

Is a daisy
still a daisy
when it floats in a jar?

Everybody tells the story of Glenn Gould. There has been praise and there has been dispraise. The dispraise exhibits complete misunderstanding. The praise is for that which seems superficial to me.
A hand placing a needle on a record.
My career, so far, has been like running through a gauntlet. A mob of managers, promoters, maestros, critics and patrons who have rained their blows on my back in order to try to beat the music down to a familiar level. Yet, even so, I can't help thinking that there must be one discerning listener – out there somewhere in the world – who can understand and appreciate what I am trying to do. Not necessarily a person who prefers my music to all the other music, no, but someone who says, Let's have it all – Let's have all of the variety of presentation and appreciation of which music is capable. Let's have every piece of music played in every way. Now where is that discerning listener? How far away is the nearest planet? How close is the nearest star? At times I come close to despair. Sometimes I think that of all the listeners in the world, the only listener with Glenn-Gould-ears is – Glenn Gould.

Chapter 5

At the University of Kentucky. A cavernous concert hall. Seven thousand people crammed into the seats. Some of them are sitting in the aisles.
Teenagers thrusting out autograph books and pens.
Playing the Goldberg Variations. The hit record they all came to hear. Loathing every note I play. Doing all the things I despise in concert-performance. Trills – octave-doublings – pedal tricks. There is something about a crowd that always brings out the worst in me. I play to their reactions rather than playing as if I were alone. I always want them to respond in certain ways. I am nervous – I am fragile – I am not in control of myself. I am performing tricks for the man in the very last row – for the tired husband who would rather watch sports at a bar – for the wife who shows off her new pearls at a cultural event. I am winning them over at the expense of the music itself.

To conduct an interview

An actor clutching a wound while giving a speech.
Lesser gods getting ready for the day ahead.
A chart which explains the Richter scale.

in which Glenn Gould

What are your thoughts about your parents?
What was it like when you were a child?
Did the relationship change over the years?

is interviewed by Glenn Gould.

A guide blazing a trail through the woods.
An archer fitting an arrow to his bow.
A fiddle being carried in a sack.

Waves of applause wash over me as I stand beside the piano. A wonderful evening, no doubt, for all but one person in the room. I am the only one here who could not write an ecstatic review.

A reporter hammering away at a battered typewriter.

Competing with my recordings under conditions that make for music at a very low ebb. Competing noise – competing motives – competing thoughts. Out of tune, spongy keyboard, an echo that muffles the sound. Feeling as if I am driving a run-away truck. I am just not a concert-performer. I shall retire as soon as I can. I would rather be alone, in my cottage by the lake, than have seven thousand people chanting my name.

He was a movie star. He was an idol. He was an angel. He was a god. His publicity barely mentioned his music at all.

"There is a dimension to Glenn Gould which goes far beyond his particular talent."

"The absorbing Glenn Gould performances reveal an interesting mind at work."

"Glenn has always understood that genius – the creative person – needs plenty of time to think. And thinking creatively can only be done alone. So I don't think I'd call him a recluse. I assume that a recluse doesn't like people. That isn't the case with Glenn. Glenn likes people – people always mention his charm. He simply seems to have decided that he just can't spare the time. He often says that for every hour in public one needs at least an hour alone – many hours alone, to judge by his practice. He eschews the cafés of Paris. The boulevards of Vienna as well. He doesn't sip an aperitif and talk of his 'art'. The great creators are ghosts to their friends. Glenn has stared hard at the facts – like Pythagoras with his famous proposition. He has deduced a simple formula – 'Creative work is never done in the midst of a crowd.' "

Came out of nowhere - the nectar is still dripping - rare gifts for the world - a man painted bars - one step above the ground - yearning for the day - a fluid expression - never an ideal occupation - invent a form.

So many people write about me. They think they know who I am. Every one of them takes an axe and blazes a trail.

One leads me along the lake. One leads me into the mountains. One takes me down to the deepest depths of despair.

Some of them seek me in the music. Some of them follow me there and get lost. Some of them never hear a single note that I play.

Every day the lesser gods had the same rock ready.
Every day he put his shoulder to the wheel.

Sitting down and writing a letter. On the table in the cottage at Upter-grove. To my manager, about the Australian tour.

A duck-billed platypus cartoon with a welcome sign.

I don't want to go to Australia. I realize that they are giving me all of my conditions. I have no quarrel with the tour that you have set up. It is ad-mirable how you have managed to protect my interests. I can appreciate how long you have spent in negotiations. The Australians have yielded on every point that I have made. The number of performances, receptions, interviews, speeches is exactly what you and I had agreed. I have always looked with favour on Australia. I was looking forward to Sydney, Brisbane, Melbourne and Adelaide. However, now that the tour is final – in black and white, so to speak – I am convinced that I simply cannot go through with it. My tour of Europe led to my breakdown. I am not clairvoyant, of course, but when I look over this schedule, I can see that something similar will inevitably happen again. My constitution will simply not endure the strain. The Australians, as you know, have been worried about my health. Just tell them they are right to be concerned. Please tell them that I am cancelling the tour.

He listened to political discussions. All the ideas that had swept across Europe. Elections debated and battles engaged. Exquisite triumphs and painful defeats. Was this a worthy way to engage with life?

Physically ill at the thought of my next performance.
Cancelling as many as I can.

"Glenn arranges his life so that nothing ever happens to him. As a result, his life is bland – desirably bland. Perhaps it's an aspect of being Ca-nadian: you want to observe, but not to be observed. Perhaps it's what artists always do: become the fly on the wall who sees everything. Who would have noticed Shakespeare as he sat quietly, in the corner of the tavern, eating his lunch? Glenn was the toast of the musical world. Ferocious conductors were eating the birdseed out of his hand. Thousands of people shouting 'bravo' and demands for a dozen encores. Offers to play at all the venues around the world. But he gave it all up for a late-night, empty studio. A cluttered apartment look-ing out on a quiet park. Look, we all take our lumps and bumps on a daily basis, but Glenn is super-sensitive. All of the greatest artists are. An everyday jolt is a Richter-moment on the Glenn-Gould radar. What to us is a fly or a mosquito is, to Glenn, a seismic assault. If he had stayed out in the world with all the pressures that he abhorred – from the producers, the impresarios, the conductors, the managers, the reviewers, the aggressive patrons, and every-one else who wanted a piece of the Great Glenn Gould – he would have been destroyed as a person. His sensibility would have been bludgeoned into the ground. A tasty feast for the musical carnivores. Battered and bleeding in an al-ley behind Carnegie Hall. And we would never have the music that we enjoy."

Blazing a trail – far-fetched looney fantasy - over my shoulder - invite a musical response - attempt to be taken seriously - feeding into the steam - a whole new piece of music - the performer's dream - what it asks of you - one's inner-experience.

Some people think of me as lonely. They even mention it to me. Some people even write about it sometimes.

What is the loneliest animal in the world? What is the loneliest bird? Surely this is impossible to know.

How could one tell whether another person is lonely? How could anyone measure that trait? The most alone person might not be lonely at all.

Throughout the climb he protected the precious fiddle.
He carried it over his shoulder in a sack.
Extreme cold, driving rain, brutal sunshine, falling rock.
The fiddle had given him ecstasy and pain.

Exhausted. My head back on a pillow. No more flying, but the train is just as depleting of my resources.

A schoolboy bending over and receiving the cane.

You know Glenn, you can't just keep cancelling every tour and every performance you don't want to do. There's going to come a point where you won't be invited any more. Right now, you're the king of the hill, but someday, when you slip a little bit, or when people get tired of buying tickets and lining up just to be told you have a sniffle and won't be there, this magic castle that you've built will melt away. These impresarios are not doing this for your benefit, you know. The maestros have their own careers to tend. Right now, you're still a life-boat in the water for classical music, but when they see you start to sink, they'll swim away.

Bach: The Well-Tempered Clavier, Book I Volume 2, BWV 854-861 / The Well-Tempered Clavier, Book I, Preludes and Fugues 9-16 / Bach: Two and Three Part Inventions, BWV 772-801 (Inventions & Sinfonias) / Inventions and Sinfonias, BWV 772-801 / Beethoven: Sonatas No. 5-7, Op. 10, No. 1-3 / Piano Sonata No. 5 / Piano Sonata No. 6 / Piano Sonata No. 7 / Bach: The Well-Tempered Clavier, Book I Volume 3, BWV 862-869 / The Well-Tempered Clavier, Book I, Preludes and Fugues 17-24 / The Music of Arnold Schoenberg, Vol. IV / 2 Gesänge for baritone, Op. 1 / Vier Lieder, Op. 2 / Drei Klavierstücke, Op. 11 / Das Buch der hängenden Gärten, Op. 15 / Sechs kleine Klavierstücke, Op. 19 / 5 Stücke for Piano, Op. 23 / Suite for Piano, Op. 25 / Zwei Klavierstücke, Op. 33 /

The performer as a puppy or a kitten. Familiar tunes – no time to practice – exhausted and adored. Not a moment to think and explore. Sentenced for life to perform the Classical Hit Parade. Endlessly repeating the brilliant, youthful puppy-tricks.

A pianist playing up to a crowd.
A ship with billowing sails.
A single bird perched on a farmer's fence.

The stratified professionalism \ the voice-leading components \ electronic tape construction \ measure their own life and work \ multifaceted-chronological concept \ complexity to simplicity \ breakdown of communications \ the totality of structure \ imperturbable self-reliance \ search for the unwritten laws.

Was there a moment when there was a break with your parents?
Did you simply see them less often over the years?
Do you regret that the sense of a family faded away?

He did not like to play in front of people.

A group of people drinking at a café.
Limousines arriving at a social event.
A celebrity being interviewed on TV.

"Glenn's health is always a matter of major concern, but neither his friends nor his doctors can figure it out. He'll parade across the stage with every ailment known to mankind. Every concert is his last – every performance is a Bernhardt-dying-swan. But Glenn is an actor wearing the mask of a hypochondriac. Put a lily on his chest and he'll bounce right back up and dance away."

A need to find time to think and to write and to develop a response to the entire classical-music repertoire. I will never find time while I am on the concert-circuit. I will never find time while running to catch a train.
Trays shaking and drinks spilling on an aeroplane.
When does Van Cliburn get time to think? When does Van Cliburn study the corpus of obscure works? When does he sit back and let the well fill up again? And George Szell and Leonard Bernstein – how do they cope with so many demands? Maestro Bernstein chomps on a sandwich as the cellist adjusts her strings. Maestro Szell does stand-up comedy to keep the orchestra loose during delays. I often wonder – when water enters a pond, does some of it sink down and mix and mingle and mature before moving on, and does some of it simply flow across the surface and go trippingly, shallowly, blithely on its way? Glenn Gould and Van Cliburn – two piano-playing, train-chasing,

airplane-hopping plyers of the concert-circuit trade. Glenn Gould or Van Cliburn – which is which? The Darlings of All the Russias in successive years. Mickey and Judy putting on a show in the barn. Pay your penny and watch the player-piano play.

The countryside was tranquil. The spring sunshine – the orange trees. The blue sea – the white sail. The painter was restless and unsure. The desire to paint such scenes was fading away.

"Glenn Gould would sell a lot more records if he'd play like Horowitz." "I wish he'd take a few lessons from Rubinstein."

"You know, it has never occurred to Glenn Gould that he might be playing out of his league. Not when he was just a student at the Royal Conservatory, playing among the older students – all potential virtuosi. Not even among the teachers there, who each had made a mark in the music world. Not when he reached the level of performance of a Liszt or a Scarlatti. He is never in awe of anyone else's style or acumen. He doesn't bow down to the great creators. He stands eye to eye with the masters of the musical catalogue – Brahms, Mozart, Beethoven, Schoenberg, Webern, Gage – and tells them where they've met or where they've failed to meet the mark. He sees Bach as a co-creator – sees himself as an also-Bach – a Bach-meister, a Bach-réalisateur. Glenn has never once been intimidated by a reputation. He puts everything and everyone under the microscope of the Glenn Gould Standard of Achievement. It's like the Glenn-Gould Olympics on the Glenn-Gould Playing Field with Glenn-Gould Rules. Read his liner-notes and his essays. Glenn has never met a giant who is taller than he."

A difficult place - glenn the invisible man - look upon things quite differently - less than he had before - strain at the utmost bounds - allowed to run away - simply protecting - faced a basic fact - what he wanted to say - isolated from one another.

The problem comes when one is written about by other people. One has a tendency to push back against what is being said that one feels is undeniably wrong.

Suppose one asks oneself what one thinks. Suppose one asks oneself what one feels. One is not going to find the answers in a book about oneself.

That is why one needs to keep oneself separate. One needs to keep one's thoughts as pure as one can. Just one tainted drop and one would have to throw the whole concoction away.

"That this arrow
might make a trajectory

around the world."

On a train between Toronto and New York. Better than taking an aeroplane. Less fear of catastrophe and more unscheduled time to think. My head against the pillow. The clicking of the rails is music to me.

A group of boys throwing snowballs at a statue.

I want to be less of a celebrity. Less praised – less revered – less deferred to – less worshipped. I don't want to hear that my music has saved anyone's life. And, if I am honest with myself: – less criticized – less denounced – less vilified – less condemned – less demonized. I don't want to hear that I should be tending the sacred flame. I just want to be a person – in the round.

The Court Musician bowed to the Count. "I am sending you on a journey. You must scour the countryside. Every apothecary and magician. Do not return without a recipe for sleep."

Straining at the chains of my confinement.
Determined that some day I will be free.

"Oh you'll never get to know Glenn. He can phone you once a week and talk for an hour, or two or three. You can feel as if your soul is bonding with his. He'll read a review, or talk of a script for one of his shows. Sometimes, he'll tell you a story – some far-fetched, looney fantasy – and leave it at that. Take those films of Glenn and an interviewer, sitting and talking beside the lake. All the questions are on one side and all the answers are on the other, of course, but very little information of import is ever conveyed. It's as frustrating as watching an interview with the Sphinx. He always gives the impression to me that he's taking in far more than he's giving out. Like he's thinking in terms of centuries while he's talking of here and now. You sense that he's there and taking part, of course, but he isn't there as himself. He's imagining what it would be like to be sitting beside a lake, and answering all those questions about himself. Oh those late-night phone calls are interesting, for sure, but I wouldn't call him your friend. Ever notice that he never asks any questions of you?"

The children came around - the accumulative experience - the size of the solar system - autobiography by displacement - an interpretive-musician - a burning, raging interest - re-write a youthful work - a failed composer - to go against the music - a dozen glenn goulds.

It's been said that I don't like people. I quite emphatically disagree. I don't see myself as suffering from misanthropic tendencies at all. Aversion is not why I don't let anyone shake my hand.

I make music for other people. Actually, I make music for myself and other people can listen in, if they are so inclined, over my shoulder, as it were. They can listen to my recordings as much as they like.

Perhaps every one of these people who write about me should spend two years in a cottage by a lake, walking in the woods – with a dog by their side – playing music in their minds without a score. At the end of it all, they would certainly not be me, nor would they know anything about me. At the end of it, they would certainly know themselves.

"It's a long way down,"
said the little bird's mother.

Reading a book in an empty waiting-room. Recommended by a friend.
A pair of crutches on a peg on a ski-shanty door.
A boy on the side of a mountain. Not in a valley – not on the top. Life in the mountains for those who do not ski. Dense fog – brilliant sunshine – driving rain. A balcony from which to view the world. Every feature covered in a blanket of clean, white snow. The sound of hooves in the clear, brisk air – the latest news in the dining room. Every day stitched to another by surgical thread. Is it possible to take one's own temperature? Is it possible to take one's own x-ray? Seven hundred pages of waiting for life to begin.

"Glenn Gould is forthright, unsentimental and deeply involved with the meaning of the music as he conceives it."
"Glenn Gould passionately pursues the ebb and flow of thought wherever it may lead."

Children
are lost
in the forest.

A poster with a piano-playing koala bear.
A hand taking a book from a shelf.
A piano with a mind of its own.

Creatures
are killed
on the roads.

What were your thoughts when your father remarried?
Did you wish him all the best?
How often do you see your father now?

Why do songbirds
never wonder

where they are?

On stage at the Wilshire Ebell theatre in Los Angeles. A concert that I cancelled earlier this year. The Art of the Fugue – Bach's Partita No 4 in D Major– Beethoven's Opus 109 – Hindemith's Third Sonata.

A baggy-pants vaudevillian with hat and cane.

Concentrating on all the wrong things. Not the joy in the work, not the perfection of the sound, but simply trying to avoid making any mistakes. I didn't want to do this performance. This is not the best use of my time. It is like playing in a museum for the portraits on the walls. So many things I want to do. Time is the only thing I own. I want to do more work like the Schoenberg documentary. I want to make programs for radio and television. I want to bring people into the music. I want some time for thinking. I want some time for writing. I want some time for simply being me. The final note of the extravaganza. A wall of loud applause. A couple of encores and I will be free to walk away. I have been predicting my end since my beginning. Sails are billowing in the harbour. I have my ticket in my hand. Has this been the final performance of my career?

Chapter 6

I have quit the concert-circuit. Told my manager to cancel all of my
future bookings. I will never play the piano in public again.

A spotlight shining brightly on an empty stage.

So – what to do with all the time that I will now have available? Everything I've been wanting to do for over ten years. I told myself that I would
only play in public long enough to be able to establish myself as someone who
does not have to appear in public at all. The dues one pays so one will no longer have to pay dues.

To live

A donkey resting quietly in the shade.
A single note on a sheet of lined paper.
An aging king offering gold in exchange for time.

in the midst of life

Why do you never talk of your mother?
What is private about that topic?
Would it not be a fitting tribute to express what she means?

by long distance.

White sails on a blue lake.
A northern cottage on a quiet afternoon.
A long lineup outside a music hall.

Sitting outside at the cottage. Reading from a pile of books. The waves
lap at the shore. Hat and gloves to ward of the chill of the morning breeze.

A young boy walking in the woods with his dog.

Until now, I haven't been myself. The travel, the receptions, the interviews – the repertoire of the Classical Hit Parade. Saplings can only bend so

far before they break. From now on – nothing but reading, writing, lecturing and recording. Radio and television will be my media – every platform that will allow me to spread the word. I want to have influence, not adulation. Farewell the travel to distant places. Farewell the agony of the stage. I haven't been myself for far too long. Now, I sit here at the cottage – water and grass, trees and books – with my Glenn-Gould mask beside me on the lawn.

Every performer needs an image. One can be famous for one's quirks. How one dresses and what one eats. How one sits and moves at the keyboard. Even facial expressions rate comments in the press.

"There is no doubt that Glenn Gould is a musical genius."
"Glenn Gould is turning the music world on its ear."

I am an aging composer! Grey at the temples and a well-trimmed beard! I am working on my opera! No more symphonies for Bernstein! No more sonatas for Van Cliburn! From now on, I will only write music to please myself! I stand up and walk across the stage! A note has just occurred to me! A very precious note! The one that has eluded me for months and months on end! The one that will open a succession of corridors and doors! I hasten to add this one new note to the rest!

An ominous silence - validity or lack of validity - sunlight and shadows - to return with you - water is trickling down - talent and originality - an hour of living - dark labels on a door - my deepest self - see far past the limits.

Oh, George Szell! Of course – George Szell! That would have to be a topic in any interrogation!
A phantom-topic if there ever was one. An event that didn't happen. A non-thing masquerading as a thing.
People ask me whether it happened. I deny it once again. Rumour has always been a machine which needs no fuel.

Other people
thought
that he was in jail.

Enjoying my freedom from the burden of my health. At least a year without so much as a tiny sniffle.
A doctor throwing away his stethoscope.
All of my illnesses were psychosomatic. They were never actually real. They were my mind admonishing my body – attempting to take its sovereignty back – raiding the ceded territory – rescinding the hated treaty – rejecting the terms of surrender. A slave-revolt against the master – attempting to

shuck the hated oars. I never expect to suffer, again, the way I did before. In the future, my health will be my least concern.

He observed the Winter Carnival. The mountain white with a blanket of snow. Skaters spinning on the glistening sheet of ice. Sipping drinks as the horses pass by with their tinkling bells. Was there merit in the life of pleasurable ease?

Knowing what I will do with all my time.
Organizing my life to suit my gifts.

I sit down at my desk! It is near the front of the stage! The one that I have been working at for years! I am about to write the note! About to write the precious note! But my daughter enters – stage left – and begins to sing! I try to remember the precious note! Now where have I left my pen? Where is the inkwell that is always on my desk? My daughter's voice is commanding! She sings as the orchestra plays! Her voice fills the concert hall! She is causing me to forget the precious note!

An archer fitting an arrow - information of import - music in their minds - a question and not an answer - a seed resting under a blanket - sleeping on the bank - bach would thank me - the clearest light of day - world inside your head - to shape the medium.

What the Maestro didn't say. What the pianist didn't reply. This has the brightest glow of all the things that have never happened to me.

The facts deserve no comment. There are none. The anti-facts have been repeated endlessly.

So I will tell you what transpired. And I will tell you what didn't transpire. No doubt you will make your choice as to what to believe.

The man was troubled
as the dog walked
by his side.

I want to record every piece of music that interests me. I want to figure out why it interests me and how it should be played as it speaks to me.

A needle riding smoothly in a record groove.

I want to record each piece as if it belongs to me. It will belong to me, in the version which I put on vinyl, for as long as that version will be played. It will be Glenn Gould's Bach and Glenn Gould's Hindemith and Glenn Gould's Schoenberg and Glenn Gould's Strauss – Glenn Gould's response to every note the composer wrote. A musical score is a question and not an answer – a question designed to invite a musical response. How disappointed all these long-dead composers must be to sit on clouds above our heads and listen in on our musical lives and to hear nothing but what they've heard many times before. The desiccation of every seed they have left behind.

Beethoven: Piano Concerto No. 5 in E-flat major, Op. 73, "Emperor" / Piano Concerto No. 5 / Beethoven: Sonatas for Piano No. 8-10, Op. 13 "Pathétique", Op. 14, No. 1 & 2 / Piano Sonata No. 8 / Piano Sonata No. 9 / Piano Sonata No. 10 / Bach: Three Keyboard Concertos, BWV 1054, 1056 & 1058 / Concerto for harpsichord and strings in D major, BWV 1054 / Concerto for harpsichord and strings in F minor, BWV 1056 / Concerto for harpsichord and strings in G minor, BWV 1058 / Canadian Music in the XXth Century / Morawetz: Fantasy in D minor / Anhalt: Fantasia / Hétu: Variations / The Music of Arnold Schoenberg, Vol. VII / Trio for Violin, Viola and Cello, Opus 45 / Ode to Napoleon Buoanaparte, Opus 41 / Variations on a Recitative, Opus 40 / Fantasy for Violin and Piano, Opus 47 / Theme and Variations, Opus 43B /

The public concert is a social and financial institution. It grew out of the musical needs of an earlier day. The musical needs and the limitations. Upon this foundation has been built a musical hierarchy. The music hall is the aging cathedral of antique sound.

Notes scribbled on a music score.
Clowns entertaining a circus crowd.
A man riding a horse in the dead of night.

The communicative ideal \ the abstract nature of his own gift \ multi-level participation in the creative process \ the listener's role \ achieve a new validity \ systemic coherence \ a magical moment \ musical perceptions \ so many moods within so short a span \ viewed in the single dimension.

Did you talk for hours with your mother on the phone?
Is it true that you used to read her every review?
Why did she insist on hearing the worst as well as the best?

He spent two years alone in the cottage by the lake.

A pile of books on a table.
White clouds in a blue sky.
A light breeze ruffling the leaves.

"As far as psychiatrists are concerned, Glenn is the clown at the circus who invites the other clowns to smell the flower in his lapel. Closer, closer, closer – what do you see? Then he gives them a squirt of water in the eye. Curses – foiled again! Baggy pants and a funny red nose. They always forget by the time he shows them the flower again."

I want to make radio programs about music. Not just me playing the music, but explaining what the music means to me.

An island with swaying palm trees and a lagoon.

And all those musicians that I've been meeting – a few words in a hotel lobby or a brief chat on a train – now I will be able to invite them to sit down at the tape recorder and tell me what the music has meant to them – how deeply the music has penetrated their bones – how they keep their heads above water while swimming in currents of fame and prestige – how they keep themselves from drowning in money and praise. All of these people are public people – with all the trappings of artistic success. To what island do you go when you want to be you?

The painter began to consider people. Old Mister Shioda, whose eldest girl had drowned herself in despair at long-lost love. Kyuichi, the young man who had been called to go and fight in the war in Manchuria. Taian, the young priest who was thought to have wasted away for love unrequited. The Soldier of Fortune with the unkempt beard and the fierce black eyes. The girl, O-Nami, whom all in the countryside thought to be mad.

"I don't know how a pianist with Glenn Gould's talent could just walk away from a brilliant career."

"I don't know how he could let so many people down."

I try, but I cannot remember my precious note! I must write it down soon or it will be lost to me for all time! My ears are assailed by crumpling papers and shuffling feet! There are some belches and some burps! I look around at the audience! Faces are glowing in the dark! I know who these faces are! Their eyes are red and their teeth are sharp! I can match each face to a scar that I bear on my person! My daughter's voice drips scorn! She sings as I frantically search for my ink and my pen! "Old man you are failing! Old man you are dying! Old man your world will simply fade away!" I stand on the stage and try to remember the precious note!

A flight of swans - takes in the patterns - all efforts to free him - driving further north - the intricacies of the wiring - music applies to more - make a trajectory - where is the ocean - a glenn-gould performance - the metaphorical significance.

I was engaged to play with the Cleveland Orchestra. The Second Beethoven Concerto. George Szell was the Maestro for that event.

I was directing the adjustments to the piano and my chair. My chair has adjustments on the legs – the piano sets up on blocks. I make no apology that the process can take some time.

The Maestro – George Szell – was quoted – a long time later – as having made a remark directly to me. "Mr. Gould, if you would simply shave a quarter of an inch off your derriere, we could get on with this rehearsal." It was printed in a seemingly-reputable magazine.

> *Years later,*
> *the boy returned as a man*
> *and ran his fingers over the bark.*

I want to write my own music. My String Quartet – Opus 1 – I am willing to put behind me. I wrote it in a little roadside grotto, at a pause in a youthful journey, somewhere along the path between the chapel of Schoenberg and the chapel of Strauss. I couldn't decide where best to spend the day.

A piece of paper, an inkwell and a quill pen.

There's more elbow grease than genius in Mozart's early compositions. He made himself into a prodigy by sheer hard work. Every minute and every thought of mine has gone into my playing career. In writing, I am at least ten years behind. I'm willing to admit – to myself – that my first flight was not all that high. My Quartet barely lifted itself off the ground. But now that I have the time, I can work at writing music the way I work at preparing a score. It will be my Opus 2 that will count.

The Court Musician rode through a rainstorm. Through the day and through the night. He pulled his hat down over his forehead. He wrapped his scarf around his neck. He only stopped so his horse could have a rest.

> Burying the demons that caused my illness.
> Exploring every topic that interests me.

A phone call to a friend.

"A person relieved of a heavy burden. Was it Hercules, or – no, let's try something else. An explorer, say, being swallowed by a snake. His torso is inside the snake and his head is still outside. Let's say he has been swallowed in his sleep and is waking up to find himself in this predicament. He has the presence of mind to extract his hunting knife from its scabbard – barely room to maneuver his elbow – and to cut through the wall of the body of the snake. An 'inside job', one might say. The snake begins to thrash, of course, but the cutting gradually lessens its crushing power and, finally, the snake succumbs to the action of the knife. The snake lies dead and the explorer slithers out – no, let's say 'he slides out' – of the carcass of the snake and achieves his freedom. Sliding past the poisoned fangs would be the most difficult manoeuver, of course, but the elation felt by the explorer would be immense."

Whether he knows me - wonder what you've learned - our existence on this earth - solitude and isolation - the rest of humankind - most luminous and inspiring order - leaves that sprout - misuse of ink and paper - how many notes - the multiple glenn goulds.

Never said. Never heard. Had such a comment been made, the Cleveland Orchestra, on that occasion, would have been looking for another soloist, at very short notice.

The rehearsal took place with good humour all round. As it was, we played the piece and I thought it went well enough. I played again in Cleveland the very next year.

I am always asked. I am always forced to deny. The most momentous non-moment of my career.

> *"That's ridiculous!*
> *During Creation,*
> *not one person*
> *recorded one note!"*

Well, I don't always expect to be taken seriously. I was having fun with So You Want to Write a Fugue? Although the sub-text – missed by many – is about how demanding the composition of serious music tends to be. It was an attempt to say, in music, a number of things about musical-form.

Patterns arranged on white paper in black ink.

The marketing people turned it down – just like some of my other ideas. The face of Columbia Records is grim – they don't see classical music as lending itself to fun. Well, it wasn't an attempt to be taken seriously as a composer. I expect to attach it, as a tag, to a recording of mine some day.

"In his Schoenberg recordings, Glenn Gould achieves his best interpretations to date."

"Glenn Gould plays with love, not just with affinity."

> *Are these*
> *the notes*
> *that have long been known?*

> *A man reading a book beside a lake.*
> *A gossip column pasted into a scrapbook.*
> *A seed resting under a blanket of snow.*

> *Is this*
> *the flute*
> *that the ancients played?*

Do you agree that the deepest relationships are the ones that we don't mention to others?

Are the ones that are with us in thought every day?

Are the well-springs of our thoughts – and our actions too?

> *How do you*
> *make a sound*
> *that is your own?*

Turning down a ton of money. Thousands upon thousands, so I'm told. More money than I could earn in thirty years.

A wheel-barrow filled with money sitting on stage.

Listen Glenn, if you don't mind me saying so, you don't want to be buried up there in Canada for very long. In the music industry, a couple of minutes is a hundred years. If you don't get back on the circuit soon, people will wonder if you're dead. The world is begging for you to come back. They already miss those stunning performances – people recall them with tears in their eyes. I see the big revival taking place down here, in the Big Apple. It's the centre of the musical world, you'll have to agree. It would generate all kinds of media coverage – the place where you made your first mark. Maybe a medley of all your best songs. We can start with Johnnie Carson – he's had Classical on before. Play a couple of tunes on Ed Sullivan – the Beatles and Elvis all over again. You know New York loves a media frenzy – the whole town caught up in the whirl. Everybody who wants attention will join the parade.

Chapter 7

We are all born into time. All of time is a river that is moving towards the sea. Every river is fed by tributary streams.

Musicians carved in marble on a Greek frieze.

What can we, as musicians, do – in the time in which we are living – that musicians of an earlier time were unable to do? What advances in technology have been feeding into the stream? Who is sleeping on the bank, with his flute lying beside him on the grass?

To remove

A shepherd whittling a flute.
A flugelhorn sitting on a shelf.
Laughing children riding on a merry-go-round.

oneself

Do you have friends among other musicians?
Did you pal around with any in your student years?
With what other instrument does the piano most accord?

from oneself.

A person playing the piano.
A rainy day in Red Square.
Flowers in a clearing in a wood.

Reading scores as I relax at the cottage. Taking a pen and eliminating every notation. Drilling down to the music at its core.

Recording Haydn: Sonata No. 3 in E-flat major.

Every piece of music has the luxuriance of vegetation. Every piece has its essence at the root. The whole pianistic tradition has been the passing-down of the flowers and the perfume. I take each note apart as I am walking in the woods. What is its value? – what is its worth? What if I had written this note? Why this note? – in this place? – at this time? Has the composer done any thinking? – or have the flowers poured forth in profusion, burst into colour and faded away? Rootless – severed – unattached? No juice – no nectar – no sap? Pressed between the musty pages of the pianistic album? Alive with roots in the soil of winter or the faded blooms of sunny summer days?

He cultivated his eccentricities. Chose his wardrobe for effect. Mixed with those who had social power. Attended events at which he was photographed. Scanned the news for every mention after every event.

"Glenn Gould's recordings are selling like crazy."
"Thousands of albums are flying off the shelves."

"You can imagine how bitter I felt. I was a pianist of quite a bright promise. I was always highly praised. Not only by family and acquaintances, but by teachers and adjudicators and many who had a claim to expertise. And then I found myself in the same class in the Conservatory as Glenn Gould. I was playing at a very high level, but when I heard this much younger fellow play – so far above my own level of accomplishment, making giant strides day-by-day – I knew that I could never play the piano in a way that would give me any peace of mind. So, I ceased to be a pianist. I took up the flugelhorn instead. So you can imagine how bitter I felt when a person with all that talent – given direct from the hand of God – walked over to a mud-puddle and threw it away."

Like a radiant beacon - a relevant criterion - don't look at the sun - one condition only - a chickering piano - i am alone - bridge-slats over the abysses - glenn gould's dreams - a need to concentrate - open up the doors.

Yes, I certainly enjoyed my trip to Russia. The Russian experience was right next to divine. The performer's dream in the clearest light of day.

The Moscow Conservatory hall began at less than half-full. Phone calls were made in the lobby during the long intermission. By the second half, there was only standing room.

There's a picture of me, I believe. Holding a great big bouquet of blue chrysanthemums. It was passed from hand to hand up to me on the stage.

"Oh I get it," he finally said.
"I know what you want me to see.
What goes around comes around – of course."

Making a move that will give me more control. Convincing Columbia to let me record in Toronto. Convincing them of the advantages over New

York. Financial advantages for them, though not for me.

Recording Beethoven: Piano Concerto No. 4 in G major, Op. 58.

Waiting for the store to close. Driving over to Eaton's for nine o'clock. Last-minute shoppers on the sidewalk going home. The helpers lugging the equipment into the store and up the elevator and setting it up. The piano on the floor beside the stage. Lid removed and the microphones in place. A few adjustments and we are ready to record. Only three or four of us present. Clear the room and lock the door. I soak my hands in the steam of my portable kettle. Last-minute thoughts as I wait for the others to check the equipment and signal their readiness. This is never an improvisation. This is a very carefully thought-out campaign. Many days and weeks and months spent living inside a score. As many as sixteen possible avenues to explore. I sit down on my chair – the tape machines are rolling – I begin to play.

He would sit and watch a lady in the dining room. With this lady he felt he was falling completely in love. From a distance, she was ideal. Up close, she was as human as everyone else. Whether to approach her or to maintain the distance between?

Thinking about the times in which I am living.
Considering how the past and present relate.

"Glenn insists that nothing untoward has ever happened to him. When something upsetting does happen, he always minimizes its existence as a presence in his life. He insists that it doesn't really matter. That it has had no ill-effect. He pulls the arrows out of his carcase and rides ahead. Not a word around the campfire of the battles that he's survived. That clash with Bernstein was worthy of Homer, but talk to Glenn and you'd never know. Glenn has plenty of wounds, but the bleeding is all inside. He's been scorched and burned and routed. Left for dead in a roadside ditch. He has knives still in his back from Bernstein and Szell. But does he ever speak against them? Glenn is like reading a small-town newspaper – all the diplomacy of a dove – keeping peace among the factions ranks above all. But it's affected how he lives. It's why he seeks a life in which nothing harsh can happen. He controls what he can control and avoids the rest. He moves his friends around like toys on a table top. Glenn's mind is like a sensitive seismograph. One false note in his music is like an earthquake to Glenn. The same is true of the notes of his life. Glenn see chaos as the alternative to control."

What are your thoughts - songbirds never wonder - certainly know themselves - the desiccation of every seed - a sound that is your own - a clearing in a wood - the true subject of art - what you want me to see - my favourite psychiatrist - the centre of the music world.

Leningrad began in a similar way. Long distance calls were expensive. A small crowd spread the word and the hall was packed.

The Russian people were starved for Western music. Anyone else would have won accolades. They were expressing something whose meaning was far beyond me.

Nevertheless it was very heart-warming. They all loved music as much as did I. Sharing such love was enough to last me the rest of my life.

The king brooded
as the stonemasons
extended the battlements.

Buying all my own equipment. Microphones, amplifiers, mixing board, tape recorders, and a device so I can play the tapes back and listen so I can decide what part of the music I want to play again. I can play a thousand notes and choose just one. I want to own the whole process myself. I want it to be the best that my money can buy. This is the payoff for living the frugal life that I do.

Recording Beethoven: Piano Concerto No. 5 in E-flat major, Op. 73, "Emperor".

Playing a movement at a time. Take 1 – Take 2 – Take 3. If it's wrong, I play it again right away. If it has some interesting things in it, I listen to the playback and make some adjustments in my sense of how it should be played. Playing – always – from memory. For months I have been experiencing the score – trying different versions in my mind – responding to the notes that speak to me. Occasionally taking a break. For the engineer and technicians, it's a very long night. Sometimes I play some Liszt to loosen up – to keep my fingers limber during the break. When the fellows come back, we start back in again. Playing, listening, thinking – playing, listening, thinking. When the nectar ceases to flow, it's time to stop. The technicians pack up and I say good-bye and go home. Back again when the store is closed. A week of recording and I have everything I need.

Beethoven: Symphony No. 5 in C minor, Op. 67 / Beethoven / Liszt: Symphony No. 5 / The Mozart Piano Sonatas, Vol. 1 / Piano Sonata No. 1 / Piano Sonata No. 2 / Piano Sonata No. 3 / Piano Sonata No. 4 / Piano Sonata No. 5 / Bach: The Well-Tempered Clavier, Book II Volume I, BWV 870-877 / The Well-Tempered Clavier, Book II, Preludes and Fugues 1 – 8 / Scriabin: Sonata No. 3 in F-sharp minor, Op. 23 & Prokofiev: Sonata No. 7 in B-flat major, Op. 83 / Scriabin: Piano Sonata No. 3 / Prokofiev: Piano Sonata No. 7 / The Mozart Piano Sonatas, Vol. 2 / Piano Sonata No. 6 / Piano Sonata No. 7 / Piano Sonata No. 9 / Columbia Masterworks, MS 7274 / Bach: Keyboard Concertos, Vol. II / Concerto for harpsichord and strings in E major, BWV 1053 / Concerto for harpsichord and strings in A major, BWV 1055 /

The musical hierarchy is, at present, quite firmly established. Its purpose is to keep the box-office sound. The most successful impresarios are the P. T. Barnums. The audiences are the crowds who flock to the circus. The touring performers are the clowns and the dancing bears.

A seismograph with a quivering needle.
A tape recorder running from reel to reel.
A painter considering his craft.

Making that mystery explicit \ a kind of unifying atmosphere \ verbatim sequential transpositions \ intense analysis \ all the music that has ever been \ motivic and harmonic relationships \ the thematic contours are identical \ antiphonal balances \ a past and a future \ harmonically-centred counterpoint.

Are other pianists somehow the enemy?
Too competitive to enjoy spending time together?
Could you and – say – Van Cliburn ever be friends?

He heard wonderful sounds as he studied the great composers.

A piano in an empty auditorium.
People rushing towards a bank of phones.
An arrow speeding towards a target.

"I don't trust Glenn when he whimpers and moans about his health. He's as healthy as you or me. He was pampered as a child. A claque of supporters smoothed his way. Now he lives in a posh apartment. A recording contract that others would die for. He can afford the best doctors that money can buy."

Farewell to the Big Apple. New York will be no loss to me. Toronto is my home. No longer will I need to take the train back and forth. The time alone will be a solid gain. My engineer can fly here whenever I wish to record.
Recording Schumann: Piano Quintet in E Flat; Piano Quartet in E Flat; The Three String Quartets.
Sitting down and listening to all of the takes. Take 1 through as many as 8 or even 9. Listening carefully over and over. Gradually emerging with a profile of the piece. Getting a sense of the shape that the music wants to take. Letting days and months go by sometimes. Seeking a version of the work that I am discovering. Making charts with a paper and pen. Bringing the music up or bringing it down – letting the music out or reining it in – cutting and splicing sections in and sections out. Creating a whole new piece of music by Glenn Gould. Bach would thank me if he were here with headphones on. Phoning

down to Lawrence Kazdan in New York. My instructions as to how to cut the tapes. When the edit is done he will phone it back to me.

Were these people worthy subjects for him to paint? What is the true subject of art? Must there be tension or tranquility? Nature as is or nature transformed? What element was missing in his head and his heart?

"There's a lady in Russia who writes regularly to Glenn Gould to beg him to go back there and perform."

"I think there's someone like that in every country where Glenn Gould played."

"A relationship, to Glenn, is like a recording which he has made. A work of art which once commanded all of his attention. All-absorbing with the need to make it right. As perfect as he could make it at the time. He can go back and listen whenever it pleases him to do so. But he doesn't carry it around with him all the time. He only revives it when he is in a certain mood. A sense of pleasure, I assume, at the perfections – a twinge of regret at what he would know to be the flaws. Perhaps a phone call out of the blue on a quiet night. Glenn doesn't need fine wines and leather-bound books. People are his luxury of choice. Each has been given a treasured spot on an exclusive shelf."

Know of the agonies - all alive to glenn - cataclysmic psychic abyss - cleared up much confusion - i know the language - to be there at all - flailing my flippers - the boy that he had lost - tattered or strengthened - brothers in occupation.

Exuberant crowds are a draught of ambrosia. A very heady brew. The same cheers, do you think, that are heard for the May Day Parade?

I never wanted their souls. I was satisfied with their ears. Such finely-tuned ears as perhaps existed in the world.

They had never heard any Bach. They had no preconceived ideas. No doubt Bach is quite familiar to them now.

"All of the moisture
would be up in the clouds, "
said the third Village Wiseman.

Making arrangements for the rental of the Eaton's Auditorium. Looking forward to recording at night when all is quiet and the store is closed. A silent building and a few technicians are all I need. Endless hours to make the music that I want to record. The word that governs my life is the word 'control'.

Recording Schoenberg: Complete Songs for Voice and Piano, Vol. 2.

Working at mastering the recording process. The best possible rendition under the best possible conditions. Every occasional flaw swept away on the cutting-room floor. Working with technicians – the best in the business. Take 1 – Take 2 – Take 3. Splicing the best notes from Take 5 into Take 7 or Take 9. Listening as they tell me how it's done. I want control over every note – total and absolute control. I want the best technician in the business to be myself. To play the console as an extension of the piano. I want to control the whole process, from the score to the listener's ear. Not one note will leave my sight until the recording is finally done. The only-maker of every note will be Glenn Gould.

The Court Musician rode into Leipzig. He directed his horse to the home of Bach. He did not seek an apothecary or a magician. Nor did he scour the countryside. "For my Master's affliction, music must be the cure."

Standing on the bank where the past stopped being the present. Constructing a bridge to cross that stream.

"So does all of this come down to his being Canadian? Is that what it's all about? Is a Canadian some kind of exotic Arctic song-bird? When he came down to New York, nobody in music even knew where Toronto was. 'Is that somewhere up near Alaska?' some people would ask. They had never seen a Canadian musician before. Must have learned to play piano in an igloo. Figured that's why he wore the gloves and the winter coat. Are all Canadians so far off the beaten track? Not caring very much what other people think? Not seeing themselves as running with the herd? Don't they care about tradition? Giving the people what they want? Giving pleasure to the people who pay the bills? Well – 'Welcome to America' is all I've got to say. He'll come around when his records no longer sell."

Never been asked before - our faults and our strengths - creativity at cost - the juxtaposition of disparate notes - trying to get a grip - haunted and tortured - the leaves are falling - the king of all this theory - let myself day-dream - their autumn-years.

It was a very seductive experience. I fully intended that I would return. I made plans to return to Russia again and again.

But reflection, for me, trumps emotion. Eye on the target, not on the bow. I was not to return to Russia ever again.

Do I see your nostrils quivering? Blue-chrysanthemum scent in the air? Are you looking around the room for a flower vase?

*"Because
it could damage
your eyes."*

A disturbance in the stream. Lawrence Kazdan has been heard to complain. I hear it by the by. A penny dropped in New York and delivered to me.

A captain pacing worriedly on the quarter-deck.

A photo-shoot for the Toronto Star. 'Glenn Gould giving instructions to an engineer.' I had another engineer fill in for Kazdan, who was working on some changes for me in New York. Now I hear that he's complaining that I didn't fly him in from New York to pose and preen. Now the waters have been most muddied, and I will never feel the same about him again. He wants to be known as the 'creative partner' of Glenn Gould. Never think of yourself, Mr. Kazdan, in your brightest, lightest dreams, as the partner-in-any-category of the pianist, Glenn Gould – Glenn Gould is the only begetter of the Glenn Gould sound. Of course, the survivors write the books, so he will undoubtedly get his way if I die first.

A cat-o'-nine-tails biting into flesh.

Dissension in the ranks! An attempted coup by the palace guard! Off with his head! Walk the plank! Erase his name from the Politburo records!

Recording Bach: The Three Sonatas for Viola da Gamba & Harpsichord.

But then – we work so well together – he accedes to my every request. Long and tedious hours making splices that I request by phone. He would be very, very hard to have to replace. I find his mutiny irritating, but he helps me to achieve the level of perfection that I want. Unlike a relationship, flaws can be removed from the recording of a piece. So – as things stand, it would be best to keep him on. I decide not to mention his preposterous yearnings. He arrives and we get right back down to work.

"Glenn Gould is using his freedom to soar like an eagle."
"What a pity if he was still chained in a concert hall."

Why are you
searching
among the leaves?

A shelf full of leather-bound books.
A stream running swiftly towards a lake.
A man talking into a microphone.

What have you lost
that you hope
can be found?

Do musicians have anything other than music in common?
Do you ever compare notes with the musician on the kettledrum?

Does a piano have much to say to a flugelhorn?

*Were you careless
or did something
steal it away?*

So why the need for such perfection? Why squeeze every note for its nectar? Why work so hard to achieve the perfect sound?

A young shepherd across the stream playing his flute.

I have no great rage at the universe. No great anger at all the imperfections that I see. But I live my life among the people who share this planet. I breathe the same air that Mozart breathed. I absorb – simply absorb – and what I absorb is reflected in the notes that I play. I am not a substitute for any other musician – not a surrogate – or a stand-in – or a temporary replacement on the team. Not the servant who delivers the missive from the king. Nor does any other musician speak for me. I deserve at least as much time at the microphone as they. I am Glenn Gould – I am a musician – as genuine as a Scriabin or a Bach. The missive that I deliver is from me.

Chapter 8

Let us have music as only we can present it. We of the 20th Century. We of the microphone, the tape-recorder and the radio.

A man in a powdered periwig speaking into a microphone.

Not Beethoven recorded in someone's memoirs – thirty years after he growled about his work. Not the music of early radio – one's living room no closer to the composer than the concert hall. Not a simple question and answer – when did you write this? – how do you write? – but a blending of thought and music – music and thought. More like a dream or a reverie than an interview. The thoughts of Stokowski today, over coffee, as we listen to his first recording, from 1917 – sixty years compressed into one brilliant floating-bubble of time. With the magic of tape and scissors, we can put the voices that we record in our day, and all of the music that has ever been recorded, into our mixing-bowl.

To concentrate

A little boy chasing a floating bubble.
A person studying a portrait.
A helicopter hovering in the sky.

on the vision

Do you have an artistic life?
Can one have such a life alone?
With no one to share your artistic hopes and schemes?

of the ideal.

A dark room with a glowing radio dial.
A newsstand with music magazines.
Farmers looking at the sky and hoping for rain.

Writing liner-notes and articles on music. Saturday Night – The Globe and Mail – High Fidelity. Studying the works and the lives of the great composers. Zeroing in on their centres of balance. Attempting to dig down everdeeper into myself.

Art of the Fugue – The Goldberg Variations – Bodsky on Bach.

What is it about Bach and the fugue? What are Bach and the fugue to me? Why do the Goldberg and I cling together and never let go? Why did Bach persist in his music when all around him had moved on to what they thought was a more appropriate form in which to do their life's work? Why did Bach continue on such a lonely path? A formalist and a man in search of a form. Music is notes – music is form. Music is form – music is notes. It is the water – it is the jar. It is the jar becoming the water becoming the jar. Why did Bach turn every thought into a fugue? Why did the fugue-form colour everything he thought? What was it that took him, every day, to work on that high and narrow ledge where daily-chaos meets everyday-control? How is it that a duck knows how to swim? How did Bach know what was required for him to be Bach?

He learned to give pithy interviews. Prepared his comments in advance. Praised the greats as everyone else did. Mozart – wonderful! Beethoven – tops! Presented himself as The Arbiter-General of Musical Taste.

"Glenn Gould edits his music as a means of providing a simultaneous variety of perspectives."

"Glenn Gould's recordings are like a movie camera shifting from close-up to long shot and back again."

I am playing the piano! On an oil rig in the Arctic Sea! I wanted Carnegie Hall, but it was completely booked! Vladimir Horowitz had taken every date! The waves are lapping at the base of the oil rig! Ravel's La Valse is always a crowd-pleaser! Weber's Konzertstuck! Prokofiev's Seventh Sonata! Scriabin's Sonata Number 3 in F-sharp minor! Litsz's transcription of Beethoven's Sixth! All the war-horses of the Classical Hit-Parade! I see whitecaps as I cast my glance to sea! It will be a two-record album! Containing every pianistic mistake! A recorded public recital! Like taking the listener along with me on one of my concert tours! The wind begins to howl in the wires of the rig! The finale will be me singing the words to the Goldberg Variations! I am the only person in the world who knows the words!

Inseparably entwined - as subtle as a cartoon - he guessed his way - concentrate on the music - focal nephritis - the note most clearly sound - a desert mirage - the making of the self - starving outside the walls - ecstasy and pain.

I spent a month in a Hamburg hotel. Essentially alone. The room-service boy barely spoke English at all.

I was suffering from the flu. Or perhaps it was just a cold. At any rate, I needed some time to myself.

I never left the room. At times I played the gramophone, and the maid would pause and listen at the door. I felt the need to move myself back to where I had been.

> *Then one day, the great Zeus came to see him.*
> *In anger, he took the lesser gods aside.*

Radio is my favourite medium. I fell in love with radio when I was a boy. Waves of sound would come in over the lake, come through rain or falling snow – to the house – to the car – to the rug on the cottage floor. What radio gives you and what it doesn't – what it tells you and what it asks of you in return. You and the radio together – creating an entire musical world inside your head.

A CBC Radio Documentary – Arnold Schoenberg: The Man Who Changed Music.

Seeking out people who feel strongly about Arnold Schoenberg. Wanting a wide selection of opinions. Wanting the interviewees to come at Schoenberg and his work from every possible side. Settling on Aaron Copland, Winthrop Sargeant, Goddard Lieberson, Istvan Anhalt, Gertrude Schoenberg and my favourite psychiatrist, Peter Ostwald. Interviewing each one of them separately. Then going back to the studio, taking my paste-pot and my shears, and building a lively conversation on an imaginary evening of Schoenberg talk. The life and the music as two hours of radio waves.

There was a lady and there was a portrait. The one was alive, but she had flaws. The other had flaws, but was canvas and paint. Ladies are ladies – art is art. Could not a better painter make better art?

> Studying the technology that is now available.
> Considering how it transforms the music of the past.

The audience seems restless! Whispering up and down the aisles! I include a few extra tricks from my concert days! 'Why the come-back?' people have asked me! Inspired by Horowitz, of course! His return has shown me the error of my ways! I have decided that I can be all things to all people! I intend to perform on stages throughout the world! I will make recordings of the entire Classical Music Catalogue! The waves are lashing against the oil rig! My plans are as wide as the oceans! I will write sonatas, sarabands, fugues! I will write symphonies, oratorios, cantatas! I will even write operas – with text in Italian if preferred! I can't believe the height of these waves! I will book all the halls of Europe! I will be touring endlessly! I will sometimes sing and make gestures, for those who prefer that way of performance, and at other times make the effort to refrain! Is the audience getting restless, or is it just me? I have convinced myself that I can do all things well! It is simply a case of managing my time!

Joy in the work - a long way down - keep themselves from drowning - centre of the musical world - eliminating every notation - what element was missing - this is the payoff - an imaginary evening - some pretty big waves - music is talk.

I renewed myself, you might say. Teleported myself back to the cottage. To where I had lived my life essentially alone.

We are all of us alone. How many face that fact? We each of us stand on the shore with our back to the town.

How many lose their sense of themselves in the tramp of the herd? How many listen to only their neighbour's sounds? How many dare dwell at the deepest core of the self?

The fiddler reached the domain of the god of music.
From the summit he could see everything in the world.
"I have come to make a request," said the fiddler.
The god of music listened as the fiddler spoke.

Writing articles on music for the newspapers and magazines. Saturday Review – Toronto Star – Musical America. All of the topics that have always interested me. The artist and his relationship to society – the composer and the search for the secret of the self.

Piano Sonatas by Scriabin and Prokofiev – Music in the Soviet Union.
Glinka – and his attempts to please the Czar. Mussagorski – and the search for the Russian soul. Tchaikovsky and Prokofiev – reaching out to the rest of the world. Scriabin – who found his music deep inside. Bach and Beethoven as political weapons – Beethoven and Bach as art for art's sake. Is one ever at one with one's fellows? – is one ever completely alone? What are the questions that keep these composers awake at night? Turn your pillow over, lay your head down, close your eyes and try to go to sleep again. The crushing demands of such powerful questions. Why should one man have to carry such weight up the hill?

Schumann: Piano Quintet in E Flat; Piano Quartet in E Flat; The Three String Quartets / Quartet in A Minor, Op. 41, No. 1 / Quartet in F Major, Op. 41, No. 2 / Quartet in A Major, Op. 41, No. 3 / Quintet for Piano and Strings in Eb Major, Op. 44 / Quartet for Piano and Strings in Eb Major, Op. 47 / Bach: The Well-Tempered Clavier, Book II Volume II, BWV 878-885 / The Well-Tempered Clavier, Book II, Preludes and Fugues 9 – 16 / Glenn Gould

Plays Beethoven Sonatas Nos. 8, 14 & 23 / Piano Sonata No. 8 / Piano Sonata No. 14 / Piano Sonata No. 23 / Beethoven: Variations for Piano / 32 Variations in C minor / Six variations on a theme in F major, Op. 34 / Eroica Variations / Bach: The Well-Tempered Clavier, Book II Volume III, BWV 886-893 / The Well-Tempered Clavier, Book II, Preludes and Fugues 17-24 /

A recording device is a means to record a moment. A moment to be relived again and again. The past is no longer the past and the present no longer the present. The two now travel into the future hand-in-hand. Recording provides a present-moment memory for all of mankind.

Water being poured into a jar.
A god shaking his fist at lesser gods.
A maid listening to music through an open door.

Notoriously controversial interpretations \ underwent an extreme metamorphosis \ accept the consequences of their own thinking \ prepares an interpretation \ the audience would be the artist \ connections are felt to exist \ the integration of line \ to establish a contact \ a century-long blind-spot \ the steady pulse of harmonic movement.

Do you know any painters or film-makers?
Any poets or novelists on the current scene?
What do they talk about over coffee or a beer?

He decided that he would take New York by storm.

A hand writing notes with a quill pen.
Technicians installing equipment in a hall.
The noises of a busy street-corner.

"Money – health – energy. Money – health – time. Money – health – endeavour. Glenn has had all of these. He's a competent money-manager – plays the stock-market like a violin. Works at his trade like a slave at a galley-oar. He's had a vision of the perfect life since he was a boy. The only precarious element here – a balancing act on a very high wire – is whether the health will hold 'til the great life's work is done."

Snow outside my apartment window. Looks like I won't be driving North. Listening to the playback of some of my earlier radio shows. Feeling the limits of the format of the radio interview and the musical retrospective. A little dissatisfied with what I have done so far.

Pablo Cascals: A Portrait for Radio – Richard Strauss: The Bourgeois Hero.

A little music – a little talk. Music as medicine on a spoon. Foreign food with a foreign taste. The inner-experience of someone far away from you. These are the instruments – these are the notes – these are the sections of the orchestra. About what Leonard Bernstein tends to do. Wanting to stretch the technical possibilities – wanting to shape the medium to do what I want it to do. Wondering what I can do differently for the Leopold Stokowski interview. Perhaps, some day, a radio documentary which isn't about a composer and his music – perhaps a radio documentary which isn't – on the surface – about music at all. A documentary which is music itself, without one single note of what the average person would consider music to be. Voices – conversations – the kind of music I hear in a diner – the kind of music I hear when I'm walking down the street.

He watched the girl, O-Nami. The girl whom everyone thought to be mad. The girl who mocked the priest who offered her wisdom from the mountain. The girl who mocked her cousin who was going to Manchuria to die. Who mocked every mood in which the painter was so sincere.

"I don't want to say anything negative about Canada, but it's not exactly the centre of the music world."

"Drop a pebble in a puddle in New York City and you're making yourself some pretty gigantic waves."

Is the oil rig sinking or is the sea rising? Come to think of it, the effect would be the same! I can see the audience whispering, but I cannot make out the words! A bird-like speck is hovering above us in the sky! A helicopter descends. My chair washes overboard in the blowback from the blades! I sink to my knees and continue to play! Actually, this is a better height for me! I begin to lose my audience! One by one they disappear! I catch a glimpse of the last of them as they scramble into the helicopter! I continue to play as the 'copter skims over the choppy waves! Perhaps it's time for the great finale! I hope the fireworks powder is dry! I sing out the words to the Goldberg, but my voice is growing hoarse! I am competing against the sound of the wind and the waves! The waves wash over the deck! I shout the final word! I stand and bow to the bark of a single seal! The waves are rising from my ankles to my knees!

Checking the invitations - other people are music - sword constantly hanging - to re-lay the keel - those artists who redesign - bach shuffled his scores - not the person or the persona - task is not the task - weave them into the fabric - a single voice.

So yes, I live alone. I have no close companions. I have many with whom I talk, but none are close.

I am not even close to my favourite composers. I can tell you which music I like and which I detest. It is their music that I admire and seldom themselves.

I wouldn't walk across the street to meet Schoenberg – or even Bach. What if he were slogging away at one of those works that are so inferior? What would honesty not compel me to have to say?

"Think twice
before you wish,"
said the magician.

The artist and the work – the work and the artist. Writing liner notes and articles for the magazines. Piano Quarterly – Contemporary Keyboard – The Canadian. More for me than for anyone else. Why do biographies account for such weight on my mental shelves? All of these portraits seem to be faced with frosted glass.

A Fetischift for 'Ernst Who?' – Piano Music of Berg, Schoenberg, and Krenek – Korngold and the Crisis of the Piano Sonata.

Ernst Krenek – producer of two hundred and twenty-five works. How is it that the soubriquet of water-bug clings to you? Will future generations see you at all? All that work and you disappear behind a fog? Alban Berg – and your note-by-note agonies. Will anyone count the candles that have been consumed by your personal flame? Will anyone bother to count the thorns in your sandals? How many drops of your heart-blood have coloured your work? Arnold Schoenberg – and the problem of the end of the line. Standing on a precipice with all your predecessor's footprints in the snow. What will happen if you step out into what seems, to many musicians, to be nothing-ness? Could you spend a quarter-century in the air? Gustav Mahler – and your piano quartet. Finding it hard to break away from the current idiom. Is this what has tied your arms behind your back? Will countless revisions lead to a final score? Richard Strauss – you who write such accommodating works for the keyboard. Why, pray Sir, have you written so very few? Erich Wolfgang Korngold – you of the legendary gifts as a piano prodigy. Writer of gratuitous, ineffectual, underpowered, redundant permutations. Why have you chosen to place such weight on the pianist's hands? Composers straining to make their music. All of them reaching towards the heavens. Standing on tip-toe for hours at a time. Why is the apple placed so high – at the top of the tree? Is the giraffe the only creature who gets plenty to eat?

The Court Musician returned from Leipzig. Through the day and through the night. He pulled his hat down over his forehead. He wrapped his scarf around his neck. He only stopped so his horse could have a rest.

Seeking avenues for ways to present my music.
Exploring form as the voice by which I can speak.

A phone call to a friend.

"Let's say there is a rainmaker. Working the farm country out in the West. Flying Jennies, those rigs are called. Perhaps a Sopwith Camel or a Rickenbacker Spad. There are plenty of those flying jalopies after the war. He goes up and shoots dry ice – from a shotgun, if you can believe it – into the clouds. Dry ice and a special prayer that had served him well-enough during the war. Anyway, they hold a public meeting. The local farmers are paying the freight. They don't have a lot of money – just enough to survive. A crowd forms beside the jail. And the fly-boy and the mayor stand up on the scaffold – that's where all the town meetings are held – and everybody tells the rainmaker their requests. So it becomes a brouhaha. Everybody pushes and shouts their requirements. 'Four inches for the homesteads north of town!' someone shouts. 'We want six inches, at least, over to the East!' 'Mind you, we don't want no raging torrents alongside the river – not like that fella give us last year! Our soil is shallow and it might all wash away!' So all this noise is going on, and the pilot's taking it in, and a little old lady comes forward. She holds up a potted cactus and she says, 'I'll put this on my windowsill tomorrow – just before you take off at dawn. I'm not worried about how many inches of rain or avoiding a raging torrent. All I would like from you is what I would call a miracle – just a drop or two of the purest possible rain.' "

What does one say - i barely know - no limit upward - an island as an idea - float on the surface - speaks but isn't heard - each one is about to speak - listening to myself - should never have spoken - a boy playing a piano.

What I have taken for myself I have taken from no one. I give the best of myself and keep the rest for me. Precisely whom have I deprived of my better self?

One's real estate is the ground beneath one's shoes. One must be on guard against letting even one inch of it slip away. It is the vantage point from which one looks out onto the world.

The world only wants to be seen as it is. It wants to be measured against what it was on the very first day. If one looks at it through borrowed eyes, one sees nothing worthwhile.

"It's a long way up,"
the little bird replied.

At home with a bowl of soup. Too excited to be able to sleep. About to create my first television special. A Canadian Broadcasting Corporation Production. The subject will be Beethoven and I will play and talk and play. Explaining what the music means to me.

The Eroica Variations – The Opus 69 Cello Sonata.

There is talk of a contract for four more music specials. Music in the USSR – Glenn Gould on Bach – Richard Strauss: A Personal View – The Anatomy of Fugue. I want to push for complete control. Complete freedom to choose subjects, repertoire, script and collaborators. I do not want to be merely the musician at whom the camera is pointed – I want to be the creator of the entire enterprise. Conceptualizing – writing – taping – directing – presenting – editing. I will do it all and all of it will be me – on tape you will have the soul of the man, Glenn Gould. Above all, the power to edit. From chaos to control by the magic of the razor and the tape. Can't wait for more talks tomorrow. Money for me will not be a factor – I can easily yield on money – I would gladly make these TV shows for free. But I must insist that I have complete control. CBC Radio has given me carte blanche – all the way. Not completely satisfied, as yet, that the CBC TV definition of control is the same as the Glenn-Gould-Dictionary definition of control. The soup is cool. I sit and sip. We shall see – we shall see – we shall see.

"Glenn Gould sees through the flesh and blood of a musical piece."
"He strips it right down to the skeleton and starts to work."

From here
the trail
leads upward.

A man trying desperately to sleep.
A fiddler climbing a mountain.
Waves lapping at the base of an oil rig.

From here
the trail
leads down.

Ever want to interact with other artists?
What the Twenties offered in Paris – in Toronto, now?
Does all of your artistic ferment come from within?

It is impossible
to stay
where you are.

All the composers that I am writing about – all the musical radio-shows – all the composers whom I am presenting on TV. These are the people of manic intensity. What is the fuel that keeps them all going? What is the drive that impels them to write? What is the flame by which they work far into the night?

A man scribbling notes in a dugout canoe.

Music is as old as the first cave-drawing. People would sit and sing at the fire – tapping bones on hides that they stretched to make a drum. Sound was as much a part of their lives as taste or sight. Different countries – different societies – different centuries – different days. Dipping the quill pen into the inkwell – horses and carriages on the street. Did even one of them ever consider that his music would be travelling through the airwaves on a quiet summer evening to the ears of a little boy who would be lying on a rug and listening intently in his parents' cottage near Uptergrove?

Chapter 9

I toss and turn on my pillow. Sleep is often the last guest to arrive. There is the music and there is the life – the welcome guest and the intruder. Is no one checking the invitations at the door?

A player-piano with automatically-moving keys.

What does the life of any of these people mean to me? I live in a different country – I live in a different time. There are waters that swirl around me that they could never have known. What could I know of the various agonies that they have endured?

To be optimistic

A young girl floating in a stream.
A young man shivering in the cold.
A sheaf of papers burning in a fireplace.

in a very harsh world

Is it true that you had a relationship with a married woman?
That she came to Toronto to be with you?
That you had a romance that lasted a number of years?

and a difficult place.

A Nazi flag snapping briskly in a breeze.
A flight of swans in a grey sky.
A group of silent patients at a spa.

Oh, young Scriabin – there you are. What a life you have had, young fellow. Always lonely – always mocked by all your peers.

A sheet of musical notes between the pages of a Latin schoolbook.

Mother died of tuberculosis. Father off to the various wars. The runt of the litter to all your half-siblings. Declared a genius by a maiden aunt. Having a terrible time at school. Smallest and weakest among the boys. Cursed, as a pianist, with having small hands. Damaged your right while practising Liszt. Doctor said you would never recover – proved him wrong. And now, you are writing an opera. Foolish enough to tell the others what the story will be about. About a fellow who succeeds – despite the rejection of his peers. A nameless hero, so you say? A philosopher-musician-poet – one whose talents and ideas are misunderstood. One who goes on to receive the accolades of all the civilized world. So, how far are you along? How many hours of grinding labour still lie ahead? A word of kindly-meant advice. Best keep silent until you can show the final score. They are mocking you, young fellow. Why insist that the future belongs to you?

If he had regrets, he kept them secret. What was the music he never had time for? Other composers – other works? There was a vast library of music just out of his reach. Suppose he introduced a new item into the program that he played? Would the managers, patrons, critics not complain?

"This cool Canadian pianist is at heart a highly romantic individual."
"Listening to Glenn Gould's music has completely altered my life."

"Someone once said to me that Glenn is missing out on all the experiences that other people see as valuable – Thanksgiving dinner with the family – the exchange of presents at Christmas time – barbecues in the backyard with friends and relatives. But Glenn had all these things all the time when he was growing up. All of those winters in Toronto and all of those summers at the lake. Glenn's not one of those missed-out-on-life artists who's art is all about the-agony-of-the-denied-ideal or the-pursuit-of-the-things-in-life-that-we-cannot-have. Glenn has absorbed all of life and moved on past it into his music. Taken it with him on his journey, like a pedlar with a sack thrown over his back. He takes his fiddle out of the sack and plays his tunes. And all the gypsies huddle around the campfire's glow."

So clear and so clean - the essential information - reading a book - a basket of blue chrysanthemums - the land of the ill - life as a water-droplet - the zoo keeper trembles - cleansing of the mind - draws the needed lines - a celebrity foursome.

Well, I didn't want to go to Israel. I just had this feeling that I didn't want to go there at all. I was exhausted from my European tour.

I had looked forward to it, for sure, when I was back home in Canada. But when words on an itinerary become cold hotel rooms and unappetizing food and draughty concert halls and pianos out of tune, one begins – as I am sure you will agree – to look upon things quite differently. I told my manager that I would like to cancel Israel completely.

"You simply cannot cancel now! You will ruin your reputation! You will never work the concert-circuit again!"

*All efforts
to free him
were in vain.*

William Byrd – Court Musician. Writer of exquisite motets. One whose lyrics are studied at Court as much as in chapel.
An axe, a chopping block and a pool of blood.
Long a favourite of Queen Elizabeth. Served you well, so far, at Court, but times are changing as we speak and it might not last. The Queen is Protestant, to be sure, despite her fondness for elaborate ritual and sumptuous music. A music lover, she, and a fellow musician, too, but she must haggle and trade at Court in her subjects' lives. She has been generous to such as you, as she has been able, so far, to be, but she has been visited, of late, by certain gentlemen with warnings dire and dark. Gossip serves as information in an age of religious unrest. Your wife has been noted as a lady with sparse attendance at church. Even you have been noted as less than fervent at times. You have been known to consort with Papists, some whose necks are near the blade. There have been certain private houses that you had been best to avoid. Your service at Chapel Royal has been suspended, as you know. Your travel-leash restricted to London, as well. Are you aware that your home has been searched? Do you know your servants well? Allegiances shift like the tides in the harbour. Small craft are caught in the ebb and the flow. The waters pour in over the lip and down they go. Let us both hope that your music can save you. These are perilous times at Court. Do you believe the Queen will protect you, if her advisors should sharpen the axe? What if the price of her nation's comfort is you and your wife?

People would ask him if he was here to stay. He would say that he was only here for three weeks. As time went on, he would adjust what he would say. He would say, "I'm only here for a short visit. Then I will go back down the mountain and resume my life".

Reading of the lives of the great composers.
Finding it hard, on some nights, to summon sleep.

"Glenn Gould is a very gentle, sensitive creature. Personal relationships, for him, can be very painful. He exhibits the questionable manners of those who are extremely shy. That's what some of the people who claim to have been hurt by Glenn can never understand. Glenn always avoids confrontation. That's why he has narrowed his acquaintances down to a very fine few. He has had the same few engineers for many years. He works with the same producers and the same technicians as much as he can. These are people, for the most part, who have never tried to become overly-personal with Glenn. Those who complain that they have been dropped abruptly – no more phone calls from out of the blue – have probably been spared what, from anyone else but Glenn, would have amounted to a major emotional jolt in their lives. Glenn doesn't tend to deliver final lines. He just slips off the stage and out the theatre door."

A life-boat in the water - simply being me - every day stitched to another - i know who these faces are - everybody who wants attention - its essence at the root - a twinge of regret - trying different versions - make better art - a bird-like speck.

The hall was draughty. My hands were cold. The piano felt like a car that was threatening to take me over a cliff.

So I drove out onto the desert. Where all the Biblical events had occurred. And I looked out over the sand and then closed my eyes.

I felt myself to be at the cottage – heard the lapping of waves at the lake. I could feel every key on the family Chickering – every key. I played the entire program, in my head, with my eyes closed, with the smells and the sounds of Ontario surrounding the car.

"No he doesn't,"
said one of his voices.
"He doesn't know
how rich or how poor you are,
how talented or talent-less,
how highly or lowly regarded by your peers –
whether you've set the world on fire
or been burned to a crisp."

Ernst Krenek – sitting on a train on a quiet siding. In the German countryside, near France. Sitting stiffly as the authorities check everyone's documentation. One day after the election of 1933.

Two railway porters exchanging the Nazi salute.

You put a black man on stage – in Weimar Germany? 'Jonny plays and the whole of Europe dances.' Your jazz opera has drawn the fury of the Nazi ire. Your works are being proscribed as degenerate art. You are a target of the party of the future here in Germany. Did you tell anyone you were leaving? Leave some manuscripts behind? Friends or family leaving the country on another train? Pressure on Austria – pressure on the Czechs. Will other countries ban your work as well? What will you do if your source of income trickles down? Sitting in a compartment on a siding near the border while a trainload of cattle-cars goes by. German authorities are checking passports – you sit stiffly in your seat. Why would you leave it quite so late to get out of town? The air has become so tight you can hardly breathe. Do you dare to open a window? Better sit upright in the seat and draw no attention. What if someone is searching your bags in the baggage car? What if they send you back to Berlin? What will Ernst Krenek's life be like in a Hitler regime?

A Consort of Musicke bye William Byrde and Orlando Gibbons / Byrd: The Firste Pavian; The Galliarde to the Firste Pavian; Pavana the Sixte Kinbrugh Goodd; The Galliarde to the Sixte Pavian; Hughe Ashtons Grownde: A Voluntarie; Sellingers Rownde / Gibbons: "Lord Of Salisbury" Pavan And Galliard; Allemande (Italian Ground); Fantasy in C major / The Mozart Piano Sonatas, Vol. 3 / Piano Sonata No. 8 / Piano Sonata No. 10 / Piano Sonata No. 12 / Piano Sonata No. 13 / Schoenberg: Complete Songs for Voice and Piano, Vol. 1 / 2 Gesänge for baritone, Op. 1 / Vier Lieder, Op. 2 / Das Buch der hängenden Gärten, Op. 15 /

All of the roles are going to change. The musical hierarchy will tumble down. Composer, impresario, manager, conductor, performer, patron, reviewer, critic – all will be shuffled and flat on the table as the technician appears on the scene. All will be levelled by future technology. Only the listener will have any status – the amateur-king.

A sword hovering over a person's head.
A group of courtiers assembling in a throne room.
A breeze caused by an invisible man.

A process of musical thought \ a handy metaphor \ a ratio of nondiatonic harmonic material \ wider range of perception \ the idealization of an impression \ the dynamic climax of the whole cycle \ essentially structural and motivational in intention \ the director's a priori scheme \ the architectural implications \ a purity of voice.

That you got along quite well with the lady's children?
That you led what was very nearly a normal life?
That you talked with the lady of getting married some day?

He impressed the greatest minds of the concert-circuit.

A family portrait on a wall.
A sandstorm raging in a desert.
A pianist performing his program to great applause.

"Glenn is a pampered middle-class dilettante. But he believes that every great artist needs a great impediment – some cataclysmic psychic abyss

– some sword constantly hanging over his head. He's a frequenter of the rummage shops of myth. That's why he tells those phoney stories about his health."

Erich Wolfgang Korngold – you of Europe and Hollywood. You have led two lives with an ocean in between.

A party with all of the usual Hollywood crowd.

Prodigious prodigy as a child. Austria's gift to all the world. Vienna dazzled by the ballet of an eleven year old. Piano sonata at age thirteen. A stunning opera at twenty-three. Youthful conductor at the Hamburg Opera House. A state professor at the Vienna Academy at thirty-four years old. So promising at such an early age. All the heritage of Europe – all its past and present and future in you combined. Displaced – as millions were – when the columns tumbled down. So you found yourself in Hollywood – writing scores for Captain Blood and Robin Hood. Plenty of cash in the bank account? Mansion up in the Hollywood Hills? Idle chatter over dinner with Errol Flynn? Mantle-piece with a row of Oscars? Swimming pool? Tennis court? Pick an orange off the tree? Take a limousine to work and another one home? So of what does your life consist – you who are living in two different worlds? Reading the news from Hitler's New Order? Night-light on with a welcome-mat for fellow Jews? Writing your real music late at night as the candle glows? What will be the words on your tombstone? Certainly 'Erich Wolfgang Korngold' – but what else? Will your oeuvre be admired when the war is done?

The girl who mocked the one who called himself a painter. He who had come here to paint and had done no painting at all. The girl who mocked him because he told her he wanted to paint her. Who mocked him when he told her that he would paint her floating peacefully, as Ophelia, in the water. Was this girl a worthy subject for him to paint?

"Glenn Gould doesn't seem to realize how much money he could make if he was to return to the concert stage."

"Somebody should hold a dollar in front of his eyes."

"Well Glenn is certainly an interesting study. I'd like to follow him around for a day. I'm sure I wouldn't see anything happen – not to Glenn at least. He always moves through Toronto as Glenn the Invisible Man. Glenn is a sponge which soaks up impressions. He takes in the patterns all around him – all the actions and all the talk – without ever taking part in it himself. He does the same when he's up at the cottage, or sitting in a diner alongside the road. He just sits there soaking it in – not saying a word. And most of the time they don't even see him – just some guy reading a book in a booth at the back. To them he isn't even a person – he's like an unread poster on the wall. They're all talking about the big raffle at the Legion next Saturday night. But they're all alive to Glenn – all their voices are making a fugue. No, Glenn's not anti-social – but he doesn't want to make friends. Other people are music to Glenn – not people at all. He's sitting and reading a score while everyone talks. Then he goes back down to Toronto with all the music and talk in his head. The creation of music is Glenn Gould squeezing the sponge."

Automatically-moving keys - squeezing the sponge - rummage shops of myth - re-hew the timbers - strips an art-form down - talk is music - control or lack of control - all voices are individual - corporeally-audible - calm is required.

The rest of the tour went smoothly. Eleven concerts in eighteen days. Jerusalem – Haifa – Tel Aviv.

Eight heaters on the stage. Bach – Beethoven – Mozart. Hat and gloves and a warm scarf – I muffled up like a bear in those draughty halls.

The best piano was in Tel Aviv. But you have to remember that Israel, as a country, was only ten years old. I played as well as I played in the cottage, although my hands were like two blocks of dancing ice.

His fingers told him
the bark had grown
and obscured his name.

Walking along beside the lake. Jean Sibelius – taking your afternoon stroll. Seven symphonies and then no more. How long has it been now since you produced a major work? The other day I heard someone say that it seems like years.

A couple of ducks bobbing for weeds at the edge of a pond.

Is there a time to let it go? To shrug it off and say that at least I've had a good run? How many symphonies should one composer expect himself to write? Mozart wrote as many as fifty – Beethoven turned out nine. There is evidence that he was working on a tenth. A laundry basket filled with notes for a major work – sitting in the parlour beside the fire – your wife is afraid to mention it to you. There have been dry spells in the past. Throat cancer – a brush with death – loss of a daughter – a wife under stress – money short – the guns of war. They say that many years ago sixteen swans flew over and you took it as a positive sign. Does the urge to create remain when you have run dry? Do you still believe in signs? Walking along beside the marsh. Do you see a few small specks way up in the sky?

He approached the Count on his dias. "I have brought you a gift, my Count. It is by far the most exquisite of all the sounds. There is a man whose name is Bach. I have commissioned a piece of music for you to hear."

Trying to keep my focus strictly on the music.

Finding my own life quite enough to worry about.

"Of course, Glenn's talent gives him a lot of lee-way. He couldn't make himself a recluse if he had to go out every day and earn a living in the day-light world. He just sends a recording out and the money comes back in. Still – grant credit where credit is due – he's the one who has put himself in that position – a musician who can live by recordings alone. And this, after he split the classical world. Half of his listeners see him as transformational – as the figure who has lifted the entire catalogue of classical music onto a whole new plane of presentation and appreciation. The other half of his listeners see him as the oaf in the china-shop who broke the precious vase. What makes it all work for Glenn is the lack of indifference. If you love him – you'll buy him and listen to him and raise your voice in praise. If you hate him – you'll buy him and listen to him and cluck your tongue in condemnation – what desecration has he committed since last I heard? Glenn is a must for every record-buyer in the classical world."

Our constant musical experience - a nightmare within a dream - what I want to know - music as a force - do we make fire - swim in your life - wonder sometimes who I am - one's life for a righteous cause - a rather spooky experience - dance across the keys.

I became a bit of a tourist. Yes me – the recluse – Glenn Gould. Drove around and saw the sights in my rental car.

Oh I admit, I turned sentimental. Donkeys – robes – sheep on the hillside. All the scenes that I had coloured at Sunday School.

And the people were extremely gracious. They kept inviting me to return. I gave them my pleasant, Glenn-Gould-is-your-best-friend smile.

"So God was living
in human time?"

You lie there in your coffin. You, who have been Prokofiev.
The hammer and sickle flag at half-mast in the cold.
Touring in the West – resenting the need to perform on piano to pay for time to compose – your health restricting you to one hour of music per day. Returning to the Soviet Union. Investigated for incorrect thinking. Denounced by your fellow musicians. Hounded by the cultural authorities. Accused by the Politburo of being an Enemy of the State. Your works banned from performance. Forced to write a Hail to Stalin – subject to government revision. And yet magnificent is the work that you turned out. Great opera followed great opera. Romeo and Juliet – Peter and the Wolf. You made your music despite their efforts to stifle you. Music that will last beyond the monolith of the state. Died on the same day as Comrade Stalin. No one to carry you from the house –

every comrade prostrate with grief – what on earth will we all do now? Bereft at the death of the Father of the State. Newspapers bordered in black. No room in the news for the death of such a one as yourself.

"Glenn Gould is working towards something that even he doesn't appear to understand."

"He's been dissatisfied at every level of creativity at which he has had such spectacular success."

Is that you
playing
the piano?

A man swirling round in a whirlpool.
A class of unruly schoolboys.
A row of awards on a mantlepiece.

Is that
the piano
playing you?

Were you devastated when the relationship came to an end?
Did you see yourself as a married man with children?
Or were you just as glad to move into the future alone?

When your fingers
are the keys,
you will know.

I lie awake sometimes and think. Byrd – Gibbons – Scarlatti. Brahms – Grieg – Bizet. Mahler – Sibelius – Scriabin. Prokofiev – Krenek – Berg. Korngold – Terry Riley – and many more. The list goes on and on. What is there in the life that makes anyone unique?
A little boy lying on a rug in front of a radio.
Who has not stubbed a toe? Who has not skinned a knee? Who has not held his hand to his bloody nose? Who has not walked in a meadow? Who has not seen clouds and trees? Who has not felt the warmth of the sunshine and breathed the fresh air? Bubbles of ecstasy – bubbles of pain. At the crossroads where the music meets flesh and blood. Every life that keeps me awake turns out to be me.

Chapter 10

Sitting in my car and waiting. A few miles north of Wawa. Just had enough momentum to drift to the side of the road.

A highway stretching for miles past a single car.

The engine quit, all of a sudden, as if I had run out of gas, yet the gauge seems to say that there's still a few gallons left in the tank. I always make sure I fill up in plenty of time. A quiet stretch of road at this time of year. A long time between logging trucks or hunters. A slight chill in the air – better not listen to the radio, in case I need the battery for the heater. Wonder how long this little hiatus is going to last? Luckily, it's not that late in the Fall. No matter – I have a score right here on the seat beside me. In fact, I have the whole thing in my head. Just the notes mind you – the unadorned, unvarnished, undistorted, un-Glenn-Goulded basic score. A little gem from the master, Bach. Plenty of music for me until someone comes along.

To make a film

A clock busy counting out the time.
Two people talking on a television screen.
A king extending a castle wall.

about Glenn Gould

What would you say is the essential Glenn Gould?
Is it the scarf and the gloves?
Is it the hat and the overcoat?

making a film about Glenn Gould.

A technician splicing two pieces of tape.
Two people planning a wedding.
A guru announcing a great find.

Being interviewed by the noted critic, Humphrey Burton. He is refusing to take the leap into future times.

A student in a dunce-cap facing a wall.

Explaining, to him, the future of classical music. How a listener will have a vast library of everything that has been recorded up until now. *How Hollywood would play it.* The listener as a composer. The best of Klemperer's Beethoven – the best of Walter's Beethoven too. Blended to make a new and better work. *To find a raison d'etre.* But Humphrey Burton must insist – he doesn't want to be an auditor-composer – he wants to be a passive listener – to hear Klemperer's version of Beethoven, from first note to last, exactly as Old Klemperer wanted it to be heard. *Re-composing Beethoven.* Well, Humphrey, what's the problem? You could still listen to Klemperer – uncut and unabridged – without any interpolations of another musician's sound. Not your own re-creation – not yourself as an auditor-composer – but only you, in your moth-eaten armchair – not playing, but being played. *Know more than the composer.* But this time it would be a deliberate choice, Mr. Burton. You would be choosing to moulder comfortably in the past.

His music shrank as his celebrity increased. He made no time to study the corpus. Music as surface, without a core. He would practice trills and cadenzas by the hour. Rhetorical statements filled his bag of party tricks.

"Glenn Gould has presented an hour of TV grandeur."
"Glenn Gould has fashioned an hour of magnificence."

I am a visitor to a distant planet! In the far reaches of the universe! Their population has not been tainted by stale ideas! I go from village to village! I am welcomed as a guru! I teach my concepts to a people who thirst for ideas! Teaching music to people who have never heard a tune! Be yourself, I tell the people, in gatherings large and small! Make every tune that I teach you completely your own! The people take to Earthling music! The people play on makeshift instruments! They hum and twitch and gesticulate as they play! Every version of each composition is completely unique!

Don't have any idea - distillation of the essence - swarm like hornets - the bottom of my brain - staggering creative possibility - totally original voice - connected or not-connected - i have decided - the children for the next ride - begins to fill the page.

There are writers who believe in traumatic moments. Moments when surely I must have veered to the right or the left. A catapult to the heavens or a dead-bolt drop to the depths.

A theory of earthquakes in the soul. Tsunamis in the blood that obliterate the landscape. The rebuilding of the psyche from a handful of primeval slime.

They scribble their charts on napkins. Scratch a curve with a stick in the sand. Glenn Gould 1– Glenn Gould 2 – Glenn Gould 3.

"Yes and no," said the old fellow.
"It's what you see and what you do not see.
Watch carefully as the children come around."

A phone call from Laurence Kazdan. Long distance from New York. A sense of urgency in his voice.

A person talking earnestly into a phone.

He says that Columbia is letting him go. Reorganizing their structure – combining departments – cutting costs. I listen to him talk. He reminds me that he has been producing my records for fifteen years – flying back and forth, from New York to Toronto and back again – working for hours in his basement to get the exact sound that 'we' want. I settle back and listen to him talk. I expect him to say that 'we' have been brothers – that Columbia is separating Siamese twins – that each of us will die without the other. The talk goes on and on. A complete review of the events of the last fifteen years. I find his distress distressful – I would never, ever, let this happen to me. I have a vision of a horse shrugging out of a harness. A horse who imagined himself chasing the wind while pulling a plough. A pause in his review of what he is calling 'our creative partnership'. I wish him luck and tell him that now, at last, he is free.

Every day he would have less than he had before. Every time the clock ticked, he had less time. Every time he learned a new thing, he was less assured. Every day that came along, there was less to do. Was less and less air moving through his lungs?

Preparing scores in my mind for future recordings.
Driving further North each time I drive.

I come to another village! There are rumours in the town! "Over the hill – in a larger city – there is another Earthling visitor! He too is teaching music to the people of this planet! The people are flocking to him in droves! He answers questions before they are asked! He has cleared up much confusion! He knows how every piece of music must be played!"

Start to sink - sails are billowing - what you do not see - match each face to a scar - my glenn-gould mask - the flowers and the perfume - a treasured spot on an exclusive shelf - responding to the notes - all things to all people - seeking avenues.

So what would be these traumatic moments? Moments that have left me so bereft that I have had to re-lay the keel and re-hew the timbers of self from stem to stern? Every atom rearranged as a new Glenn Gould?

The cupboard was bare of my favourite food? The book I was reading seared my soul? The end of my childhood on the day my old dog was put down?

The competitions, two years at the cottage, the New York debut? The trip to Russia, the month in Hamburg, the day on the desert in Israel? The Bernstein affair, the Hupfer imbroglio, the rumoured insult from Maestro Szell?

> *"What are you thinking,*
> *Your Majesty?"*

A letter from Peter Ostwald. My favourite psychiatrist.
Two men lying side-by-side on a psychiatric couch.
He is getting married. Herein is enclosed a photo of his intended. I must send them a wedding gift. I should phone him up and tease him. I shall chide him for keeping the lady a secret from me. I shall ask him whether she will prove to be a distraction. He is already a full-time doctor – and an amateur musician, as well. Do we not give up as much as we add to our lives? He has pursued me for many years. He fancies himself as a fisherman and Glenn Gould as Moby Dick. He is, by far, my favourite analyst – my favourite fish on a hook. We met in San Francisco, after one of my concerts there. I reeled him in while he was fishing for me.

Schoenberg: Complete Songs for Voice and Piano, Vol. 2 / Six Songs, Op. 3 / Eight Songs, Op. 6 / Two Ballads, Op. 12 / Two Songs, Op. 14 / Three Songs, Op. 48 / Two Songs, Op. posth. / Händel: Suites for the Harpsichord / Suite No. 1 in A major, HWV 426 / Suite No. 2 in F major, HWV 427 / Suite No. 3 in D minor, HWV 428 / Suite No. 4 in E minor, HWV 429 / Glenn Gould's First Recordings of Grieg and Bizet / Grieg: Piano Sonata / Bizet: Premier Nocturne; Variations Chromatiques / Bach: The French Suites, Vol. 1 / Suite No. 1 in D minor, BWV 812 / Suite No. 2 in C minor, BWV 813 / Suite No. 3 in B minor, BWV 814 / Suite No. 4 in E-flat major, BWV 815 /

The way we view the past will be profoundly altered. Now the past can travel with us – side by side. Suppose an old-timer speaks of Stokowski, and the sound of '17. I can put that sound on my turntable, more than fifty years after that sound was made, and that sound will be happening now – as fresh as the buds on the trees – a sound that can never be played in a concert hall. I was born in 1932, you see, but from the moment the turntable turns, my personal memory-experience will include that musical-moment-experience of 1917.

> *Village wise-men debating a salient point.*
> *A camera tracking its subject relentlessly.*

A hand reaching in the dark for a phone.

Texture of themes and counter-themes \ the disembodied idea \ erected a more stable keel \ to dissect this music \ the very best metaphors we have \ compelling structural simplicity of form \ the penultimate variation \ clarity of definition \ effort of re-creation \ the most incredible complexity.

Is it the fact that you live alone?
That all of your thoughts are private thoughts?
That even your friends are always wondering who you are?

He was given a contract to make any record he liked.

A pianist practising his craft.
Two people watching a merry-go-round.
A person putting a record on a turntable.

"Ever get a glimpse into that bag of pills? He's got a whole bloody pharmacy in there! Valium – Aldomet – Inderal – Librax – Indocin. Red – orange – yellow – green – blue. Glenn's the self-medicator, par excellence. Now – whether all those pills have enabled him to do what he's been able to do, or whether he would have done twice as much without them, maybe only Glenn himself would be able to say."

The people I phone to fill up the night-time. There have been dozens of them I am sure. People who attach themselves to me and don't want to let go. Do they realize that all they have to say is 'no'?
A radio dial glowing warmly in the dark.
I like to share what I am thinking. I phone them up anytime from about eleven in the evening to as late as just a few hours before the dawn. That would be for the ones in my time-zone. For the others, I never bother to check the time. They either want to listen to me or they don't. I never ask them what they are doing. I never ask them if they have time. I play them music which I am enjoying. I read them a passage from a book. I read an article on which I am working. I tell them of future plans I might have. I never ask for their opinions. I never want to know what they are thinking. I never act on what any of them might say. The phone is my night-time radio station. The topic is always 'Glenn Gould'. It costs me a fortune, but it's well worth paying for. I have a list of names and phone numbers. Once in a while I add a new name and cross one off.

He watched the girl but he could not paint her. He wanted to paint her but he knew that something was wrong. What was missing in every scene? Was it missing in the girl or was it missing in himself? Why had the paint remained in the paint-box all this time?

"Glenn Gould not performing in public is like Nijinsky not dancing."
"Or Shakespeare not writing or Beethoven not composing."

"The other guru tells us that he has made a great find! It is the original manuscript of a piece of music that he calls the Goldberg Variations! In this manuscript are many notations! Hundreds and hundreds of notations! For the first time, the guru says, we can know what the Maestro Bach was thinking as he wrote! Now, the guru says, we know exactly how the Goldberg must be played!" I lose my appetite for teaching! I thank my hosts for their hospitality! I turn my back on the distant planet! I climb back into my spaceship and blast away!

The lapping of the waves - two blocks of dancing ice - a purity of voice - left me so bereft - the most private public-person - woven into the life - omnipresent in the sound - boy who tinkles the tunes - what is inside the man - long-term trend.

Scan the minefield of his daydreams. The wreck on the ocean floor of his hopes. Probe the nightmares that lie down with him at night.

Was his mother a little too strict? Was his father a little too lax? Was he an only child who yearned for a massive brood?

Did he cry when fish were battered? Did his piano fall off a truck? Did any mishap skin his elbow or scrape his knee?

"But the rain
already falls upwards,"
said the fourth Village Wiseman.

I find it best not to deal with people. I find it best not to deal with people at all. Every meadow is a potential battlefield.
Two duellists, back-to-back, in an amicable mood.
Menuhin – Burton – Ostwald. Kazdan – my engineer. My cousin – Jessie Greig. My father – whom I seldom see anymore. A certain female with whom I established an illusionary bond. All the technicians who come to see themselves as the 'creative partners' of Glenn Gould – the ones who are so convinced that they take his crude, pianistic noodlings and make them presentable. Fresh waters when we meet – great gulps of refreshing rapport – then the inevitable drop of poison in the well.

The music was exquisite. It soothed the sleepless nights. The Count would call for his variations. Rub his temples and close his eyes. The music would drive his troubles out of his mind.

Getting away, as much as I can, from other people.

I am happiest, when alone, in the North, in my car.

A phone call to a friend.

"Let's say a person is accustomed to playing the piano – any tradition-al piece, recreationally, of course– and then he suddenly stops playing. At first, he assumes he is going deaf – we can think of Beethoven, perhaps – but then he realizes that his piano is playing – not notes all of a sudden, but – playing words! He begins to play again, and to listen closely. Yes, the piano is playing words! Words he can barely hear, mind you, but certainly these are words! No longer does his piano play the notes of yesteryear. Now, would it not follow – logically-speaking – that this fellow would feel an obligation – by whatever personal honour-system to which he presumably adheres – to at least attempt to address this issue and to try to ascertain the actual words which his ear can barely hear? He plays – he listens – he plays. The words are tantalizingly near. The mystery of the other side of the membrane. By what means, then – help me think, here – might he go about this quest – this Sherlock-Holmesian Ar-gosy – in pursuit of whatever El Dorado is pressing to be heard?"

What is the form - awareness of inner-ness - a dream within a night-mare - a placid island - a block of stone - ten times ten - controversial musical figure - another glenn gould - visible on the surface - all blend together.

Oh, I could write it all myself. It was written before I was born. Every generation wears hand-me-down baby-shoes.

I could scribble a couple of paragraphs. Send it off to Hollywood. 'Tormented genius smashes brick wall to attain the sublime.'

Marlon Brando, James Dean, Montgomery Clift or some other ago-nizing thespian. A charismatically brooding young actor with pain in his eyes. 'Piano music dubbed-in by the real-life Glenn Gould.'

"Well I might just
 take one little peak
 anyway."

I have an ideal relationship with the great composers. I spend every waking moment with them, but I've always been grateful that I don't have to know them personally.

A row of painted portraits on a wall.

I do not have to talk with them on the phone. I do not have to meet them in coffee shops and diners. I do not have to live with them in my home. Mozart – the temperamental. Beethoven – the irascible. Strauss – the haughty. Schoenberg – the fierce. I wouldn't hail a one of them if I saw him across the street. However, I can know them – I can know them – sometimes better than they can know themselves. Through their music – note by note and movement by movement, with my magnifying glass – I can see very deeply inside their minds. I can penetrate to the core of their private selves – see them strain at the utmost bounds of being human – see the intricacies of the wiring of their brains. I know the language in which the great musicians think.

"Glenn Gould is one of those artists who redesigns each form in which he works."

"He strips an art-form down to its core and builds it back up again to suit his purposes."

A feeble hand
puts pen
to paper.

A space ship landing in a cloud of dust.
A music score with no notations.
A diagram scratched in the sand.

A feeble
hand
touches the keys.

That you are the most private public-person of our time?
That you only communicate in the language known as music?
That people feel an essence-to-essence connection with you?

Every ear
in the village
hears the sound.

Sitting in my car alongside the road. Not too far north of Wawa. Still light enough that I can see my watch.

A man in a car, with his eyes closed, humming a tune.

The sound of an engine, labouring up the hill. A glance in the rear-view mirror – a truck at last. He'll be picking up speed on the flat as he moves towards me. It's twilight – pull the switch and turn on my lights. I get out on the pavement and flag him down. The driver puts on the air-brakes and pulls over to the side. He rolls down the window and leans out as I walk along beside the length of the truck. He looks down at me with concern. The truck is throbbing, so he has to raise his voice. Hey, there Bud! Looks like you could use a little help! Any idea what caused her to quit? You're a long way from civilization! You get this late in the year, there's not a lot of traffic! You shouldn't oughta be out here all alone! Oh, it's quite all right, my friend – I've been fine-tuning the performance of a score.

Chapter 11

The come-back offers keep pouring in. Why do some people only see money when they look at me?

A pianist on stage with a clutch of blue chrysanthemums.

Hey Glenn, just give a listen – hear me out. I see the whole thing gathering steam – moving on over to Europe. You know they eat up culture there. You'll play for all the crowned heads we can gather – they'll all show up if they get in free. Hundreds of interviews in every country. Radio – newspapers – television too. We can book these massive venues – lineups forming around the block. Say the Opera House at La Scala – the open theatre at Pompeii. Then who knows where we can take it. You'd be a sensation again in Russia – there was a time when they were crazy about your Bach. Does China have concert halls? You'd be gigantic in Australia and Japan.

To listen

A technician tuning a piano.
A person reading a script.
A girl in a painting of a play.

simultaneously

Do you ever wonder what the future will think of you?
Does posterity mean anything to you?
Do you cast your mind ahead to the coming years?

to more than one conversation.

A group of people meeting in an office.
A Greek hero rolling a rock.
A court musician playing for a count.

Making a television special with Yehudi Menuhin. Mozart's K. 333

Sonata – Beethoven's Opus 34 Variations – Berg's Sonata. Music and words – words and music – music and words.

Two comedians bantering shtick on a TV screen.

Handing Yehudi my script. What is this?, he asks. *Wish Beethoven were here.* The script, I say – I wrote it for us both. It is a distillation of what we both believe about music. I thought it would save us from babbling superficial inanities – that it would take us right to the core. We can make it sound spontaneous if we rehearse it a couple of times. *To go against the score.* I am very disappointed when he balks at reading my words. My words of his ideas, if he could just see. *Between two worlds.* We go on and do the taping, and Yehudi speaks his own words, but somehow the target is missed – he misses what my script would be sure to provide. *The real spring.* In the end, I am left with somewhat of a disappointment. Idle chatter on a topic, but not idle chatter distilled. The program doesn't quite say what I want it to say.

He lost his luggage in Barcelona. He lost his nerve in Budapest. Nervous prostration caused him to increase his consumption of pills. A month alone in a quiet hotel. A kindly doctor helped him climb back onto the concert whirl.

"For Rubinstein and Horowitz, the music is a means of giving people what they already know they want."

"For Glenn Gould, the music is entirely something else."

"I believe that the loss of Glenn's mother was a great blow to him. He learned to play the piano on her knees. She taught him that he was special, but would never allow the word 'prodigy' to be heard in the house. That's why it's always the work with Glenn – never the trappings of stardom. She played the organ in the church and Glenn has said that his whole style of playing is organ-inspired. That is undoubtedly the explanation of the life-long attraction to Bach. But you can search his interviews in vain for references to his mother. That's just Glenn, of course – Glenn is always so close with what matters to him most. His mother was the touch-stone of his life. He would call her up and read her the reviews. Even the negative ones – she insisted on hearing them all. No, you'll never get Glenn to talk about his mother. One of those influences that is all too deep for words. He lived at home until he was twenty-seven years old. I don't think he turned against her – just stopped seeing her so often, that's all. Whatever estrangement there was in the later days was simply Glenn's detachment from himself. He is estranged from his father in much the same way."

The true glenn gould - one thing is for sure - it's not for me - my theory is controversial - natural-born showman - thought is levelled down - seal it in a locket - building interpretations - trapped in time - i have convinced myself.

Oh the Gould-Hupfer imbroglio! What in the world could I say about that? Well, I needn't say much about that kerfuffle, as so many people have already commented – or let us better say 'speculated' – on that topic already.

It all took place at the House of Steinway in New York. I had been using Steinway pianos for many years. I knew exactly how I wanted my piano tuned.

The Chief Steinway Technician, on that particular day, was a Mr. Hupfer. I wanted a hair-trigger action and he wanted something soft. He kept saying that he kept Horowitz in tune.

"This task is not the task I meant for Sisyphus!"
This procedure has merely wasted a thousand years!"

CBC television is not as amenable as CBC radio. They don't believe in carte blanche as a management style. I tag along for these Glenn-Gould specials – the ornament rather than the engine under the hood.
An office boy fetching coffee for the people in charge.
Perhaps I'll give them an ultimatum – Glenn Gould in or Glenn Gould out? – Glenn Gould not participating or Glenn Gould all the way? The bottom line – for me – is control or lack of control. Am I the writer, the director and the editor – or just the boy who tinkles the tunes? I'm not happy with just a little dab of Glenn Gould.

Was he well or was he ill? Death on the mountain or death in the town? Life on the mountain or life in the town? The smog of the flat-lands or mountain air? Was this the life he was born to live or another life that he found himself living instead?

Seeking control over every aspect of communication.
Lacking the patience to let anyone else take the lead.

"The role of Glenn's father, I would say, has been to hover in the shadows – to make sure that the spotlight shines on Glenn. He made the famous Glenn-Gould chair, of course. Legs cut short – adjustable latches on the sides. It enables Glenn to play the way he does. After that, his father fades right out of the picture – like the stagehand after he fiddles with the chair. Remember that Churchill is famous – not Churchill's chauffeur. Family has always been the curtain behind Glenn's career. Of course there has – of late – been an estrangement. Glenn refused to attend the wedding. His father has remarried, as you might know. Glenn cannot accept the fact that his mother has died. As far as the family goes, I would say that Glenn was in the family but not of it. Glenn is a safe-cracker who leaves no fingerprints. He's left his family far behind and escaped with a personal choice of the family assets. Aside from the chair

– which Glenn refuses to have re-upholstered – you won't find much evidence of his father clinging to Glenn."

The ever-narrowing range - brilliant puppy-tricks - in black and white - a spotlight shining brightly - i make no apology - a very precious note - never an improvisation - blue-chrysanthemum scent - let us have music - returned from leipzig.

We went into the Steinway office to sort the matter out. Mr. Hupfer was summoned and followed along behind. I settled into the chair in front of the desk.

Suddenly, I received a tremendous blow on my left shoulder! It felt like a sledgehammer coming down with terrible force! It drove my shoulder down and my elbow against the chair!

I looked up and looming above me was Mr. Hupfer. One of the Steinway people jumped up and came between us. "Mr. Hupfer was just being friendly with you, Glenn! – Mr. Hupfer didn't mean to do any harm!"

"All my life I have been plagued with earthly demons.
Let me play my fiddle here, on the summit.
If I could play for just one hour without the demons
I'm sure I could make such music as has never been heard."

Besides, television has proven to be no more than a fleeting flirtation. Music doesn't seem to mate well with the nature of TV – a camera searching for where the notes are coming from.

Violinists sawing vigorously with their bows.

To watch a flugelhorn-player play his horn is not all that enlightening. What is the flugelhorn-player thinking as he plays? There are seventy to a hundred people in an orchestra. What is every one of them experiencing as the music rises and falls? What of the person who has one note on the kettledrum? Music as people – people as music. The camera should follow these people onto the bus as they leave the studio. What would they say to a tape recorder on the kitchen table at home? I sense that radio, as a medium, has more for me.

The Mozart Piano Sonatas, Vol. 4 / Piano Sonata No. 11 / Piano Sonata No. 15 / Piano Sonata No. 16 / Fantasia in D minor, K. 397 / Beethoven: Piano Sonatas, Op. 31 Complete / Piano Sonata No. 16 / Piano Sonata No. 17 / Piano Sonata No. 18 / Glenn Gould Plays Hindemith's Piano Sonatas 1-3 / Piano Sonata No. 1 / Piano Sonata No. 2 / Piano Sonata No. 3 / Glenn Gould Plays His Own Transcriptions of Wagner Orchestral Showpieces / Prelude to Act I (from Die Meistersinger) / "Dawn" and "Siegfried's Rhine Journey" (from Götterdämmerung) / Siegfried Idyll / Bach: The French Suites, Vol. 2 & Overture in the French Style / French Suite No. 5 in G major, BWV 816 /

French Suite No. 6 in E major, BWV 817 / Overture in the French style, BWV 831 /

Music is now all around us. It has moved out of the concert hall. Tie and tails are mouldering in the closet – concert tickets confined to a drawer. Radios, record players, televisions – there is one in every room – are playing every day and everywhere. Music grew out of our daily existence – it is the sound of our daily existence once again.

A wheelbarrow filled with money.
A pianist holding a trembling hand.
A boy sitting on his mother's knee.

A protective shield around humanity \ inter-movement relationships \ developed an infallible instinct \ a collection of tape segments \ encoded and decoded \ harmonic structuralism \ a greater quantity of thinking \ decision-making capacities \ stripped to its fundamentals \ the problem of the analytical double standard.

Do you think that the future will judge you?
Will they see you as a person at all?
Or will they think of you as a name on a record sleeve?

He was booked for concerts in every concert locale.

Two older people getting married.
A person on a balcony in the mountains.
A musician playing a kettledrum.

"I see Glenn's health as his major failure in life. Maybe all of us have one flaw – one major area of concern which we've allowed to run away and jump the fence. For Glenn, his major failing is the management of his own health. He has squandered his youthful freshness in a brew of potions and pills. Every attempt to make himself healthy has made him worse. Sometimes his hand will tremble and he always tries to cover it up with a smile."

A recurring sense that there is more than just the music. Not instead of the music, no, but a sense that the music applies to more than just musical sound. A sense that the musical-documentaries are not enough.
A small boy making castles in the sand.
I sit alone in the truck-stop diners, but I don't feel that I'm alone. What do the truck-stop diners have to do with Beethoven or with Bach? What did the choir babble about while Bach shuffled his scores? What did the people say in the taverns while Beethoven ate? I can't believe that the music was separate

from the weave of the lives. The heart throbs and the lungs pump – there is rhythm in all that moves. There is talk and there is music – the music is talk and the talk is music. The rhythms of both are woven into the life. I can't see confining myself to only musical-biographies. Surely the greatest musicians weren't thinking of themselves alone. Their eyes looked both inward and outward and realized that the territory was much the same – that the one is the mirror-image of the other. I want to make radio-documentaries. I want to record the sounds of the voices that I hear each day. I want to record the music of life – to find a shape for these ideas. There has to be a way to make this work.

Who was this girl, O-Nami? The painter wondered as he watched her, day by day. Was she Ophelia, the girl of Denmark? Was she Ophelia, the girl in the play? Was she Ophelia, the girl in the painting of the girl in the play?

"Someone should tell Glenn Gould to keep it simple in those talks he gives on music."
"Just tell us one single thing at a time and go on from there."

"I left my husband for Glenn. I moved to Toronto for Glenn. I even uprooted my children. It was love – I'm sure it was. I thought we were perfect for each other. We would take long walks and talk. There was a notion, between us, of marriage. Glenn was wonderful with the kids. But as time went on, I knew it wouldn't work. We never lived together. That was impossible from the start. Glenn habits were so eccentric. Glenn's apartment was like a fortress. Glenn flirted with domesticity, but he was taken up with his music. After I moved away, he would phone me repeatedly. We would visit once in a while, for short times. He was so sure that it could work, if only I would come back, but I always said no. There was no sense in the two of us being naive."

Could feel every key - his fingers told him - the project shapes itself - every atom rearranged - an essence-to-essence connection - looked both inward and outward - this fellow bach - thinks it's something else - form-as-process - penny in the grass.

Numbness, in-coordination, shoulders out of balance – such debilitating symptoms went on and on. I had to make a number of cancellations. I wondered whether I would be able to play again.
I consulted a number of physicians and chiropractors. I spent a month in Philadelphia, in a cast. Mr. Hupfer's actions had threatened my whole career.
The Steinway company defended Mr. Hupfer. They said that he didn't mean any harm and therefore no harm had been done. They said he was simply protecting what he thought of as the Steinway sound.

"That this arrow
might make a trajectory
around the world."

I have to solve the radio dilemma. I don't want to be an actor, playing parts. I don't want to be a voice on the radio.

A spotlight featuring a microphone on an empty stage.

I don't want Glenn Gould to be there at all. Oh, the essence of Glenn Gould, but not the person or the persona. I have to figure out how to be omnipresent in the sound, but not there – corporeally-audible – at all.

The Count was curious as to the man who wrote the music. "Who is this fellow, Bach, who has written my variations? Of what court is he an adornment? For which noble does he spin such well-wrought gold? How can he write such exquisite music? Will I get to meet him one day?"

Thinking of ways by which music can transcend music.
Wondering how to bring that idea into the light.

"So why did Glenn Gould leave the cottage? Why did he start driving further and further North? Quiet motel rooms along the highway in the remotest logging towns. Why didn't he keep the cottage when his parents got old? Well, there are people who go on treks – pilgrimages to sacred sites. Not just to Katmandu or Machu Picchu, but to the lairs where the famous people live. Try to catch them in their backyards – cooking a steak on the barbecue – or dozing on a hammock with a book on their chest. Or maybe practicing the music that has charmed the world. Hoping to have the conversation of a lifetime – become a go-fer in an extensive entourage. So it was fame that did him in. The family cottage wasn't private anymore. Glenn left the cottage when the cottage stopped being North. Fortress-apartments in Toronto – quiet motels on up-country roads. North is the matching of place and self. Glenn just wants to be left alone. North has been harder for Glenn to find as time has gone by."

The mind as deep and quick - the world in which he is living - as thick as the leaves - gargoyles have a purpose - pick a voice - the audience sits and waits - lifeless, old and tired - locked within these grooves - matter of contention - rites of passage.

I launched a lawsuit against the House of Steinway. My lawyers filed it in the District Court of New York. When you are right you have to take things all the way.

There were dollars mentioned in the suit, but the number of dollars was not the point. It was Steinway vs. Glenn Gould. It had become a case of who should control the sound.

It is the pianist who plays the piano. The piano should always be tuned at his request. I wanted Steinway to admit that Mr. Hupfer was wrong.

Just then,
a little breeze
nudged the branch
which held the nest.

Sitting down, once again, with the life of Bach.
A sliver of moonlight on the surface of a shimmering lake.
An old, leather-bound tome. Silent for years, on a shelf in my parents' cottage. One of many purchased through a book-club, years ago. So often the urge to read it, with the moths outside the window, at three AM. The pages are dark and the print is fine. People used to read such books by candlelight. The question is, as always, with Bach – to read the life without the music? – to read the life while the music plays? – to put the life back on the shelf while the music speaks?

"Glenn Gould's problem is that he is such a rare and refined individual."
"There are very few people – when one contemplates the music world – with such an exquisite sensibility as himself."

Hold the seashell
to your ear.

A television set in a living room.
A car driving along a northern road.
A person alone in a hotel room.

Hear the sounds
of far away?

Do you ever judge yourself?
Do you go easy on your transgressions?
Are you a stern and merciless adjudicator of your slightest misdeeds?

Hear the sounds
of many thousands
of years ago?

Working towards an idea. Breasting the waves with the honing-sense of a lumbering tortoise.
A clutch of eggs throbbing at night in the salty air.

What is it for which I am searching? I have a feeling that it includes everything that I have been interested in – everything that I have been studying – everything that I have been working on for all these years. I have faced a basic fact: that I am not a great creator of musical works. I am not going to stand beside my idols. I am not going to be another Mozart or another Beethoven – another Strauss or another Schoenberg – not even another Grieg. Where is the ocean in which I seek to swim? A hatchling – flailing my flippers in the sand as I sniff the air.

Chapter 12

Always the come-back question. All the concert stages are carpeted with dollar bills.

A body stiff and cold on a slab of stone.

The whole world loves a come-back, Glenn. It'll be billed as a Lazarus Event. Your records will sizzle like hot-cakes – best-sellers all over again. This thing will make every one of your records pop. We could play up all the agony – how you hate to appear on stage. It's called the Judy Garland Syndrome – lots of people would pay just to see if you fall apart. Then you go back to your rustic cabin – way up there in the backwoods of Canada – and count your new pile of dough. You owe it to the music – you owe it to your fans. Your bank-account will be bulging at the seams. So why are you laughing, Glenn? What seems to be the hold-up – what do you say?

To transcend

A group of people watching a person drown.
A man talking into a telephone.
A hand placing a record on a turntable.

the frailty

Are you the kind of person who never feels despair?
Do you ever feel you have reached the end of the line?
Are there occasions when you feel there is no way out?

of nature.

Hands racing up and down a keyboard.
A page with vertical and horizontal lines.
A winking sign on a northern motel.

On a train heading North. The Muskeg Express. From Winnipeg to

Churchill, Manitoba.

A single kayak in a pack of drifting ice.

Not the North, but the Edge-of-North. Where the road and the railway stop. After this, you need a dog-sled for the mail. *The clear, clean water.* Riding along in the dining car. Looking out at the stunted trees. The Canadian landscape unrolling, mile after mile. *In the cockpit with the pilot.* A man sits next to me at the breakfast table. The niceties, and then we start to talk. Eight hours later, we're still talking about the North. What it is and what it means. *This is going to become impossible.* Isolation and deprivation – end of the road and points beyond. The sense of the self when caught in a snowstorm –what is left when the blizzard subsides. *A one-time tourist.* Are you going North from Churchill? Not an iota of a need. The idea of North is the thing that grips me. Solitude and isolation – the Northern experience as metaphor. I can be isolated while driving through Toronto in my car.

And he was tired – always tired. Another airport – another hotel. Another draughty concert hall. Another piano that was brutally out of tune. Another night alone after all the aficionados go home.

"Glenn Gould is the only pianist who has set himself a standard of perfection."

"For all the others – good enough is good enough."

It is a pleasant summer day! I am a tourist at Niagara Falls! The Horseshoe Falls, on the Canadian side! Thousands of gallons a minute pour over the waterfall! Plenty of tourists are enjoying the view! The mist makes our faces wet! I mingle among the crowd! Suddenly there is a noise! Someone shouts and many others begin to shout! They all point up-river! "There is someone in the water! Being swept towards the falls!" I press against the railing and try to see! A man is flailing in the water! He is sweeping towards the precipice!

Far from any implication - if rain fell upwards - movie of my career - an atomic-age monster - a publicity bonanza - taken in and made orthodox - dispensing wisdom in the agora - this chain of command - as from a cloud - ran his fingers over the bark.

The Bernstein-Gould affair? What to say? – What to say? Well, for me, it's just the facts and nothing more.

It was the New York Philharmonic, conducted by Leonard Bernstein. The piece was the Brahms D-minor Concerto. The guest pianist, on this occasion, was Glenn Gould.

You give to the music what is best in yourself. You give to Brahms what is the best of Brahms in you. I planned a Brahms at which even Brahms would be surprised.

One day,
he stood out
in the wind and the rain.

What to do next is always the question. To whom should one turn for inspiration? The great composers? – the great conductors? – the great pianists? On whom should one bestow the most esteem?

A group of worshippers bowing before an idol.

Every musician presents a pattern – a pattern of mind and heart and soul. A grid on which one's life can be plotted and compared. A touchstone by which to measure one's thoughts and deeds. Rubinstein and Horowitz divide the world between them. Whose rock is rolling faster down the hill?

He took flowers to those who were dying. Plumped up their pillows and put them at ease. Took them for walks along the trails. Took them to see the places where they would soon rest in their graves. Was he doing this for these people or for himself?

Taking a train through the swirling snows of Manitoba.
Feeling akin to the people who live up here.

I look closely at the man with the stricken face! The man who is battling the raging current turns out to be me! I am swept towards the Horseshoe Falls! I cannot believe the power of the current! I flail my arms but there is nothing I can do! I hear the crowd above the roar! "He's going over! There's no escape! The current's too strong! There's nothing we can do!" I am about to go over the precipice! Suddenly I feel something! It feels like a twig or a branch! I clasp my hand and my shoulder is given a violent wrench! The water pours over my head as I tighten my grip!

A recipe for sleep - a single bird - endure the strain - the dues one pays - a succession of corridors and doors - carefully thought-out campaign - it could damage your eyes - not a simple question - i renewed myself - exploring form.

I phoned Mr. Bernstein from time to time, to explain what I had in mind – for my Brahms was going to be a very unusual interpretation. He said that he would keep an open mind. Finally, at our first rehearsal, I played my Glenn-Gould Brahms – unspectacular, minimal, subdued, contemplative, introspective, contrapuntal – a fresco as opposed to the usual trumpet-blast.

Well, Mr. Bernstein disagreed. He preferred, he said, a more traditional interpretation – more up-tempo, more conventional, more an expected Bernstein performance, more what the Philharmonic audience had always enjoyed. I told Mr. Bernstein that there was no room for compromise.

Perhaps he considered turning me over to an assistant-conductor for the performance. That is often what maestros do when faced with such concerns. But we rehearsed the piece together, as I had planned.

The dog was untroubled
as he walked
beside the man.

A contract with the CBC. To make a radio documentary. To be called The Idea of North. But not a standard radio program like the ones we hear all the time.

A recorder threading tape from reel to reel.

Not with an A-B-C progression. Nor a travelogue or a report, but rather an exploration – an exploration of an idea. *To correlate the disparate views.* Choosing five individuals – five people with varying experience of the North. A civil servant – a nurse – a sociologist – an anthropologist – a surveyor. *A place to dream about.* Five people who know the warmth and the cold of the North – five people who have never met – five people who are isolated one from another. *To read the signs.* Meeting them singly, in hotel rooms – a tape-recorder on a chair. Asking each the Glenn-Gould questions – isolation? – elation? – despair? What were you when you entered that kingdom? – tattered or strengthened when you returned? *The metaphorical significance.* The tape recorder turning – a single voice in a quiet room. Five people who don't know one another – exploring the landscape in which each has lived completely alone.

Bach: The Three Sonatas for Viola da Gamba & Harpsichord / Sonata No. 1 in G major, BWV 1027 / Sonata No. 2 in D major, BWV 1028 / Sonata No. 3 in G minor, BWV 1029 / Beethoven: Bagatelles, Op. 33 & Op. 126 / Bagatelles, Op. 33 / Bagatelles, Op. 126 / The Mozart Piano Sonatas, Vol. 5 / Fantasia in C Minor, K. 475 / Piano Sonata No. 14 in C minor, K. 457 / Piano Sonata No. 17 in B-flat major, K. 570 / Piano Sonata No. 18 in D major, K. 576 / Hindemith: The Complete Sonatas For Brass & Piano / Sonata in F for French Horn and Piano / Sonata for Bass Tuba and Piano / Sonata for Trumpet and Piano / Sonata in E-flat for Alto Horn and Piano / Sonata for Trombone and Piano /

The narrowness of the concert program has given way to a vast historical repertoire. Music that couldn't pay the bills is now ours to record. The creation of a vast recording archive is now ours to achieve. Works that were once confined to obscurity will be our constant musical experience in future days. The whole history of music for everyone to explore.

An old fellow digging a hole.
A girl marvelling as a virtuoso plays.
A person talking into a tape recorder.

Shared awareness of inner-ness \ form-as-process experiments \ preserving a structural autonomy \ editorial control \ revealingly antithetical properties \ all judgements are relative to a given fundamental \ the extra-musical perspectives \ individualized information concepts \ an interpretive conviction \ cerebral exclusivity.

That you are trapped in a cage?
Whether your own or some other craftsman's?
Something preventing you from realizing your dreams?

Every concert-patron worshipped at his feet.

Ice freezing on the windows of a train.
Water tumbling over Niagara Falls.
A rustic cabin in a clearing in the woods.

"Glenn worries about his hands. I know he does. Always devising tests and exercises. Always probing to see whether the hands are still up to task. The fastest hands in the world of music – the most precise in the pianist's trade. He's always alert for any signs of slowing down – any indications that he might be losing his edge."

Arthur Rubinstein is working his magic at the piano. Oh, of course – it's the A-flat Polonaise. Every eye in the hall is on Arthur Rubinstein. Arthur's eyes are busy sweeping the concert hall.
A poster for a Hollywood romance.
He is looking for control, control, control. To persuade – to take hold – to dominate. To reach out with his music and caress the listener's soul. His face, at times, looks like he is praying to God. But wait – it's something else. There is a female in the audience – one who has taken his practised eye – and he is playing to only her. And if there were many such damsels, why then he would have his choice, and work his spell for her – and her – and her. The only profession where your muse must pay to see you play – a diamond choker applied to her neck as you hand her the bill. He has been doing this now for over sixty years. All the stamina of a man of half his age. If his hands are slowing down, it has not been noticed. Not one of his muses has ever complained at all.

The girl was beautiful as she stood in the morning light. Holding a dagger in her hand. Three times the dagger flashed across her chest. Many had told him that she had gone mad. Was this girl a worthy subject for him to paint?

"I tuned in to Glenn Gould's radio show and there was very little music."
"Somebody told me that human voices are music to Gould."

I am hanging on for my life! The water pours over my head! I am hanging from a twig or a branch! I twist myself around! I reach past the branch and get a grip on a rock! Now my two hands are my ticket back to life! I try to heave myself up above the torrent! Suddenly, some of the members of the crowd leap from rock to rock and stand above me! "Help me!" I manage to cry, but they raise their feet and begin to stomp on my hands! Many more pour over the railing and come to their aid! I twist my head and look to the railing! It is myself with a stricken face! People jump up and down on my hands! All I can do is watch in horror as I cling to the rock!

The smells and sounds of ontario - sixteen swans flew over - a vast library of everything - the weave of the lives - get to meet him - a hand clutching a branch - what is the form - an interpretive conviction - the gauge seems to say - a new glenn gould.

The hall was filled for the Thursday-night concert. I am always alone when preparing to play. I was soaking my hands in hot water when Mr. Bernstein appeared.

Did I mind if he spoke to the audience about what we were about to do? He showed me a note on which he had written what he wanted to say. Was it all right with me if he told them that we disagreed?

I went out on stage and sat down and played for fifty-three minutes. I played the piece my way. It was a Glenn-Gould performance through and through.

*The man
was downcast
at the boy that he had lost.*

A motel in the village of Wawa. The north shore of Lake Superior. Fishing – mining – timber. Gas station and coffee shop.
A vacancy sign blinking on and off.
A thoughtful drive north from Toronto. A chance to get some thinking done. Audio-tapes on the back seat of the car. *I got there by mistake.* Five voices from north of Churchill – five impressions of the great beyond – five instruments playing their solos on their balconies at night. How to weave them into a fabric with a single theme? *A most minute measurement.* If all voices are individual – if all individuals are one – what is the form in which each voice can best be heard? *You could see the bottom.* Listening to the tapes – five separate interviews. Reading the typed transcripts – one by one. Reading them over

and over. Separate – together – fused – apart. *A long, terrible, trying trip.* The grit of the day – the lilt of the dream. Isolation – deprivation. Escaping North? – escaping South? *The last shimmer in the sky.* A documentary disguised as a drama – a drama that thinks it's something else. *Experience that we now face.* What is the form by which each voice will remain a single voice? What is the form by which five people will seem to be one?

"I know very little about him, my Master. Beyond his name and the piece of music, I have nothing to tell. He offers his music, but not himself, to all and sundry. He asks your Honour for nothing in return. He does not even bother to give his music a name."

Standing where the dog-sleds wait for passengers.
Projecting my mind as far North as it can go.

A phone call to a friend.
"So let's say an old fellow is digging a hole. He is using a round-mouth shovel – he's been digging all his life. Not digging a grave with a spade, like they do in the movies. This would be clay, so it isn't so easy-going. The trick with clay is that you get a pail and keep pouring a little water into the hole as you go along. Clay when it's dry is like digging concrete – clay when it's wet will slice like butter – so digging clay, you always want to keep it wet. He's down to about waist-deep when a neighbour comes by and asks him what he's digging for, and the old fellow says: 'I'm going to dig my grave and bury this here gold coin. This coin will act as a comfort in my old age.' He takes a gold coin from his pocket and holds it up. 'I'll put it down at the bottom, and fill the hole again, and when I need it, I'll know the gold coin will be there for me.' 'What a foolish thing to do,' says the neighbour. 'When you are old, you'll have aches and pains. Your muscles will shrivel up. You'll be confined to a bed and you won't be able to dig, and the coin at the bottom of your grave will be no use at all.' 'I'll tell you what,' the old fellow says to his neighbour, 'when I get old, I'll lie right here, beside my grave, on a makeshift cot. I'll tell my story to passing strangers. I'll tell them all about my gold coin lying six feet down. If someone digs it up for me while I am still alive, then life will still be worth living; if everyone waits for me to die, I'll be better off dead.' "

Three or four different lives - telling him the story - an actor playing a role - proportion and distortion - contrapuntal simultaneity - every pianist faces - young and boyish again - the boy I used to be - vary a note or two - the known exterior world .

Afterwards, there was a terrible brouhaha. The musical press kept the whole thing churning for months. Everybody in music had an opinion as to what had transpired.

Someone said that Mr. Bernstein had betrayed a colleague by agreeing to accompany my performance and then going out on stage beforehand and washing his hands. Someone said that Bernstein had stabbed me in the back – publically and cold-bloodedly – on stage. Someone even predicted that such unprofessional treachery might well drive me out of performing in public again.

So what did I think about it all? I said publically, again and again, that Mr. Bernstein showed me the speech ahead of time and asked if it would be all right with me if he went out in front of the audience and delivered those words. I have always said, time and again, when anyone has asked, that if that's how he felt about it, that he should go right on ahead and make the speech.

"God was not living in this world!
God was living in eternity!"

The return of Vladimir Horowitz. A triumphant return to Carnegie Hall. *A concert ticket pressed in an album of photographs.*
Away from the concert stage for ten long years. Tickets scalped at record prices. Aficionados lining up around the block. Mme. Horowitz serving hot chocolate in the frigid air. Thunderous applause as the great man bows and takes his seat. Playing all the familiar pieces. Scriabin's Étude in D-sharp minor – Chopin's Ballade No. 1 in G minor – Rachmaninoff's Piano Concerto No. 3. Every dart in the Horowitz repertoire dipped in honey. Dynamic contrasts – overwhelming fortissimos – delicate pianissimos – thunderous chains of double octaves. Every piece a perfect copy of the one he used to play – every sausage in the casing of uniform size. The music sounding so much more exquisite after such a long wait – piano tuned by Mr. Hupfer to the Steinway sound. The tape machines spinning out a two-record set – immortalizing every cough and sneeze. He has booked every hall in every country in the world – a classical-music travelling-circus enterprise. The applause ecstatic – the bows humble – the encores extending endlessly. The couple lingering as the applause lights up the stage. "Vladimir so missed his public," says Mme. Horowitz, "during the long years he was absent from the stage. Music simply isn't music when played alone. He will perform in public until his dying day."

"To Glenn Gould, music is the language of the deepest level of human emotion and thought."
"More significant than fire as a force that we have wrested from the gods."

Find a penny
in the grass –
bright and clean.

A group of people viewing a mountain grave.
A person alone in a hotel room.
A hand clutching a branch in a waterfall.

Spend it at
the corner store –
a treat for the day.

Do you feel that you are always moving forward?
Do you always know the direction in which you are bound?
Will there be a day when you know you have reached your goal?

Better keep it
if it was coined
when you were new.

The CBC radio studio in Toronto. Editing The Idea of North with Len Tulk. Overseen by Janet Sommerville. A few uneasy moments – all along, I have insisted that I have free rein.
A family listening to the radio in their living room.
Five weeks to the scheduled broadcast. Working night after night after night. An idea finding its shape as it eats up the time. *This north-man-ship thing.* Five people who have never met – taking part in a conversation as if they are sitting in a diner, together, in Wawa – as if they are all sitting together on a northern train. *Making nothing of it.* Speaking separately – speaking simultaneously. Speaking for oneself – speaking for the group. *How one can best attain an idea.* The voices weave in and out – the voices are each distinct. When is a group not a group? – when is an isolato not an isolato? *The real truth about the North.* The unseen person in the group will be Glenn Gould. I am the one who weaves them together, but none of my questions will ever be heard. *The train is about to leave.* None of the speakers will ever be named – they are the voices of the North. They are speaking as representatives of ideas.

Chapter 13

Busy – happy – healthy. What more could an old fellow want? All the aches and pains that come with this model, though. I was fresh on the shelf in 1932.

A young boy running his fingers over the keys.

Counting on the mind to pull me through. Though the body wastes away, the mind can always continue to grow. It feeds on emotions and ideas. In my garden I have both – some at harvest, some at seed. The trick is to cultivate every patch of barren ground. I am walking towards the grave with a sack of seeds slung over my shoulder. Happy to foil those sages who are predicting my demise.

To seek compensation

Two people sitting in a restaurant.
An old fellow taking his daily exercise.
A patient checking himself with a stethoscope.

for pain

Ever think of writing a book about music?
Explaining just what music has meant to you?
The Anatomy of Music, by Glenn Gould?

in artistic order.

A car moving along a northern road.
Fishermen bringing in a catch.
A boy playing a piano in an empty room.

The Idea of North has been a breakthrough for me. I now have my own idea-form. Form as meaning – meaning as form. Glenn Gould – the Inventor of the Contrapuntal Radio Documentary.

A group of people clinging to a rock.

Not a word of lecture or summary – imagery without explanation – autobiographical for me. *A perfect example of anarchy.* I am a contrapuntal person – not a straight-line narrative kind of guy. *A hard thing to contemplate.* Perhaps a series of documentaries. The idea pleases the CBC. But what might be a good topic? Solitude – separateness – isolation. Other people – self. *I know where I am.* An item in the newspaper. A cabinet minister on TV. A day or two in a northern motel room. A working script as a series of questions. *The only good on the face of the earth.* Back to Toronto and packing a suitcase. Consultations with the CBC. Then off to Newfoundland with a microphone in hand.

His hair grew grey. His stature increased. He was the lion of the concert halls. Dowagers fought to entertain him. His repertoire never changed.

"Glenn Gould has an enormous talent for music as well as iconoclasm."

"History might well conclude that Glenn Gould was the only sane musician of the century."

"As a psychiatrist, I would have to say that Glenn Gould is the one that got away. I had dinner with him at the Benvenuto, when I was in Toronto. He was gracious, shy and courteous as we sat there and he talked – mostly about music – what he liked and didn't like – but I couldn't help but think of his phobias. Fear of the cold, fear of infection, fear of pneumonia, fear of the air-conditioner dripping over the door. He was dressed as if it was winter and here it was August weather outside. Gloves and an overcoat as we walked along the street. Oh, I would have loved to have been Glenn's partner in probing his mind with him. No, the dinner was to thank me for recommending a specialist of the throat – it had nothing to do with psychiatry at all. You know, it occurred to me to wonder whether he was exaggerating his well-known eccentricities. I still wonder whether he was putting on an act. He hardly ate a thing – said he wasn't hungry at all. It was he who'd suggested the restaurant – it wasn't me. So, I broached the forbidden subject. Said it as casually as I could. Said it might just ease the sleeplessness that he had mentioned as being a problem. Of course, I assured him of complete anonymity. Told him that no one need ever know. He never said a word – let me finish my dinner in silence. Not one more word about music or anything else. I usually order pie, but he got up and went to the counter. He paid the bill and told me he had a lot to do. He told me to take my time and turned and walked out the door. He used to phone about once a month, for a couple of years at least. After that dinner, I never heard from Glenn again."

Cannot be easily told - working my way inside - go further north - an enormous rock - dancing on a string - a disservice to humanity - made this claim - life-time of exploration - the maker took the time - a single note.

You know, two of the places where I spend most of my time are the seemingly-opposite landscapes of a recording studio and the diners which I encounter along the roads. The quietest place one can find when in the city – the noisiest place one can find when in the country. A monk alone in his cell – a monk in town.

I spend long days and nights in motel rooms, way up north of Lake Superior. I study the scores of whatever music I would like to play. I take long drives along the lake and listen to music in my car.

> *He watched intently as the children clambered on.*
> *Every child was on a unicorn when the music started to play.*
> *He watched most closely as the children came around.*

Always the question of what to do next. From what spring to draw my purest inspiration?

A conductor punching a ticket on a train.

The railway platform at Frankfort am Main. On the Amsterdam-Vienna run. On my way to perform at the Vienna Festival. An old man stretching his legs at the pace of a snail. Leopold Stokowski! The Maestro! The man who makes the recordings! The man who has pioneered the art. The man who has been recording since 1917. The history of recorded music in his grizzled crown. I wonder whether he knows me. Has he heard of me at all? Are we brothers in occupation? Or, more likely, father and son? I wonder if he will conduct at the Festival. The old fellow makes his walk from lamppost to lamppost. Straight ahead – never a glance or a look around. What does one say to one so aloof? A priest in the courtyard of a seminary – scriptures in hand. How does he reach such a tranquil state? How find peace in such a maelstrom of travel and noise? Perhaps by rebuffing any such eager acolytes as myself. The whistle sounds – he approaches the train. I drop my ticket at his feet. As he pauses, I bend over and bow down.

One day he went out for a walk and was caught in a blizzard. He fell asleep as the snow was coming down. A nightmare within a dream within a nightmare. A dream within a nightmare within a dream. When he awoke, the snow was calm and he was alive.

> Checking my fingers for nimbleness and elasticity.
> Feeling the mind as deep and quick as it's ever been.

"You know, I think it's a common phenomenon that, at a certain stage in life, a person will consider that he – or she – could have led three or four different lives. That – looking back – a person can see that the opportunities that required the choices – or the disappointments that closed the doors – were all, more or less, equivalent at the time. That the fork – or forks – in the road weren't the big and the small, or the significant and the insignificant, but were rather, more or less, about the same. Not so with Glenn Gould. There was no fork in his road. No Glenn Gould 1 or Glenn Gould 2 from which to choose. Glenn only saw one road – straight ahead and moving upward – and he followed that trajectory from his early days as a child. Just think about it for a moment – look at the cabdriver, the doorman, the insurance salesman, the haberdasher – can you imagine Glenn Gould being anything other than what the world now knows as Glenn Gould? Glenn Gould knew he was Glenn Gould from the moment of birth."

Music buoy him up - measure their own life and work - a worthy way to engage - a little roadside grotto - masquerading as a thing - as human as everyone else - the only begetter - sixty years compressed - all of us alone - becomes a brouhaha.

I have always enjoyed just sitting and listening in diners. A few of my favourites are here, in Toronto. The best ones are at the truck stops along the shores of Lake Superior and Georgian Bay.

And I just sit there, with a glass of milk, and listen to the voices. And sometimes someone will speak to me and of course I speak as well. But I would always prefer to listen than to talk.

Do you know one of the nicest things that has ever been said about Canada? Perhaps you've heard it before. 'It's a place where they leave you alone.'

"When the peasants are all dead,
we will have no more need for these walls."

Taping voices in Newfoundland. People who've never met. Thirteen voices seems a good number.

An empty fishing dory knocking against a dock.

A whole month on the rock. An exhilarating experience. *A very powerful force.* An island in the Atlantic. A separate history – a separate life. Connected and not-connected to mainland Canada. *It seemed so to us.* Awash in currents, cruel and kind. How much does one surrender? – how much does one keep for oneself? *What we can substitute.* The abandoning of the outports – old people moving to larger villages – young people leaving on the ferry – fishing villages left behind in enveloping fog. *Something within.* A chance to work in stereo – an audio-metaphor. *The smell of that Scottish heather.* Human progress – human loss. Thousands of years of storm and sunshine – thousands of catches – thousands of wrecks. Taping all of the moods of the waves as they break on the shore. *Some purpose in life.* An island between two cultures.

What to appreciate? – what to disdain? A month of interviews on a rocky is-land. A conductor making probes with a microphone.

Bach: The Six Sonatas for Violin and Harpsichord / Sonata in B mi-nor for violin and harpsichord, BWV 1014 / Sonata in A major for violin and harpsichord, BWV 1015 / Sonata in E major for violin and harpsichord, BWV 1016 / Sonata in C minor for violin and harpsichord, BWV 1017 / Sonata in F minor for violin and harpsichord, BWV 1018 / Sonata in G major for violin and harpsichord, BWV 1019 / Glenn Gould Plays Sibelius / Sonatine No. 1 for Piano in E major, Op. 67 / Sonatine No. 2 for Piano in E major, Op. 67 / Sonatine No. 3 for Piano in B minor, Op. 67 / Kyllikki, Op. 41 /

For a performer such as I, these are very exciting days. I can study one piece of music for a month or more. I can study each composition – every note as a separate gem. I can prepare an interpretation, record that piece on a cer-tain day, and it will be available to listeners all over the present world – even listeners who are waiting to be born. I can then decide what other great work to explore.

A person looking down at ants on the ground.
A hand holding out a bag of coins.
A person standing at a fork in the road.

The psychobiographical process \ postpones the moment of reckoning \ some form of nondiatonic or extradiatonic contrast \ catholicity of repertoire \ the dream was more like a nightmare \ inspired interior monologue \ if music were always reduced to its skeleton \ the omnipotence of the enlightened mo-ment \ the accumulative experience \ isorhythmically organized fermatae.

Your thoughts on music in the morning?
Your thoughts on music throughout the day?
Your thoughts on music as the sun goes down?

They couldn't believe the way his fingers flew on the keys.

A handsome grey-haired matinee idol.
A monk sitting alone in a cell.
A gardener scratching at the soil.

"Oh Glenn talks about his health – of course he does. 'It's my greatest single fear at approaching old age.' But then he'll pull a curtain across. 'I'm a hypochondriac! Of course I'm fine! The critics search my recordings in vain for a single flaw!' After you talk to him, you wonder what you've learned."

Leopold Stokowski. A penthouse in New York. Looking down on the reservoir in Central Park. Here to interview the Maestro for a radio-documentary.

Two people meeting on a bridge above a chasm.

The Maestro shuffles off to order us each a drink. He bridled noticeably when I said that I only drink tea. I wonder if he remembers me from Vienna. About my playing he has never uttered a public word. What to ask the aging Maestro? I have pondered this for days. He is eighty-three years old. He's been recording for fifty years. He is equally at home on the concert stage. Such a long career to set beside my own. What has he never said in an interview? What has he never been asked before? I barely know what it is that I want to know. I have a whole sheaf of questions on familiar topics – 'tradition in music', 'fidelity to the score', 'the composer-performer relationship' and a dozen more. Information that Stokowski admirers will want to know. But this is irrelevant to me. What I want to know is what is inside the man. Will he talk about the world in which he has lived? – will he talk about the world in which he is living? – how to draw him out to talk about himself? He comes back with the drinks. Wine for him – tea for me. He sits down across the table. The technician gives the signal. The tape recorder starts to turn. I set the sheaf of questions aside. The aging Maestro looks across at me curiously. I lean forward and tell him the story of one of my dreams.

He watched the girl as she met the Soldier of Fortune. The two of them face to face on the scrubby hillside. Some coins in a bag in her outstretched hand. Clutching the dagger which she had hidden in the folds of her robe. Was this girl a worthy subject for him to paint?

"I have to admit I don't understand Glenn Gould's contrapuntal radio shows."

"He makes them as noisy as the office I work in all day."

"Perhaps they'll say, some day, of Glenn Gould, that he always wanted to be a composer – and he wasn't one. That might come to be the central fact about Glenn Gould. He always talked of being a composer. Just look at those early interviews. A major reason for his retirement from concert life – to devote himself to the writing of major works. And what has he produced? Well, an honest trifle or two. His claim to greatness is 'So You Want to Write a Fugue?' There are many great recordings – and every one is stamped 'Glenn Gould'. Glenn is one of the all-time greats as a pianist. But the question that intrigues is as to what Glenn thinks of it all. The record goes silent on that topic soon after Glenn retires. He ceases to talk about his own writing. Dozens of interviews and writings, all on composers other than Glenn. A thread that goes silent in the weave. Perhaps the saddest situation in life is to spend one's time yearning for a life that one is not living. Perhaps the saddest person in the world is Glenn Gould."

Set the world on fire - completely altered my life - just the notes - to share what i am thinking - a new and better work - territory was much the same - music can transcend music - a treat for the day - equivalent at the time - no one will ever know.

I discovered the recording studio when I was just a boy. No one was watching me as I played. A great big empty room with just me and a microphone.

For the first time, I was able to be myself. I could eliminate the mistakes that undermined me. I could present to others the best of what I was.

You know, the task of every human being is to determine the ideal distance between himself and every other person on the earth. For me, that required a microphone and a recording. For me, that was not a concert hall.

> *"Do you mean to say*
> *that the rain leaves the earth*
> *and goes up to the clouds?"*
> *asked the fifth Village Wiseman.*

Interviews with my characters. Not seeing them as people at all. The need to shape my documentary. The need to shape my fictional form.

Lobster traps drying in the sunshine.

But why?, I ask the lady. Why do you feel the need to escape? It isn't that I need a specific answer. I need her to think on the deepest questions. I need her to descend to the deepest rift. I need her to dig right down to the bedrock beneath her feet. *Be still and know*. She gets angry at my questions. Why would I ask her again and again? Finally, she turns on me with fury. A female lion pursued to her den. *There's no isolation.* All of the thoughts she has never admitted all come pouring out in a rush. Her anger at Glenn Gould is her anger at isolation. Her need to get away from Newfoundland is her need to get away from the self. *The necessity of doing our best.* Isolation is her cage. The microphone is a sharpened stick. She is magnificent as she sits on the sofa and snarls.

The Court Musician did not tell what he knew. That Bach was no longer in favour. That his eyesight was failing and his health was poor. That the other musicians looked askance at the music he wrote. That he wrote the music it pleased himself to write.

Weighing the challenges for one who is nearing fifty.
Feeling nowhere near the end of my personal road.

"The intriguing thing about Glenn Gould is that he keeps making these radio documentaries. He interviews people – one on one. He practically goes to the ends of the earth to find their burrows. Then he asks them all kinds of questions about how they manage to handle living a life of isolation. Then, when he gets all of these voices on tape – in the laboratory, as it were – he knits them all together, by splicing them, electronically, into some sort of a semblance of a community. Now what in the world would a psychiatrist make of that?"

Know very little about him - trapped in a cage - a worthy subject - the persona behind the mask - suffered agonies - isn't quite himself - eager to tell you all - perched on a rock - larger purposes of creativity - the greatest puzzle.

I live alone among my fellows. I tune my music to the human voice. The music and the voices are the same.

Every voice has a singular value. Voices are speaking all at once. Every single voice is appealing to be heard.

So I'm alone among the many. An individual in a crowd. Taking in and giving back as best I can.

> *"If you do,*
> *it could be*
> *the last thing you'll ever see."*

The Stokowski apartment. Many floors above the reservoir in Central Park. Looking down, one is put in mind of an ant.

A distant planet with a footprint in the dust.

I finish telling the story of my dream. One of those dreams that always seems to be lying in wait. The Maestro sits there silently. He raises a mottled hand and takes a sip of wine. Is the interview essentially over? – will he be guarded and obscure? – is the Maestro the kind of man who never dreams? The Maestro puts his wine glass down and begins to speak. He speaks of the size of the solar system. He speaks of our existence on this earth. *This distance is enormous.* Of war and of famine. Of our faults and our strengths and our struggles. *Endless space and endless mass.* Of the artist's aspirations. Of how he strives to improve his art. *There is no limit upward.* Of new ideas and possibilities. Of music as a force. *The deep roots of a great oak tree.* The Maestro takes another sip. My head is buzzing with ideas. How to present this to the listener? What would be the ideal form? Should this be framed or should this be the frame? *New possibilities and new ideas.* He speaks of the cave man and the birth of ideas. He speaks of love, beauty and order. Yes, he speaks of destruction too. *It is interesting because it is life.* He speaks of what is happening on this earth. He speaks of the music that he hears when he walks in the street. *The immense mass of possibilities.* Then the interview is over. Maestro

Stokowski has had his say. Time has moved along quite rapidly. The lights are on in Central Park. Headlights help to define its borders. The people are too small to see from this height.

"Glenn Gould has been remarkably consistent over the course of many years."

"He thinks in centuries every minute he is at work."

Stand as close
to yourself
as you can.

A person talking into a microphone.
A waitress with a smile and a glass of milk.
A messenger who declines to tell what he knows.

Stand as far
from yourself
as you can.

Would this be your true autobiography?
Would this be a true biography of you?
Just Glenn as front and back covers with music inside?

Your truest self
will be somewhere
in between.

Editing The Latecomers. The studios of the CBC. Thirteen characters who have never met, in a simulated community. Brought together only on tape.
A telescope scanning slowly along a shore.
The lioness who spoke to me fiercely. The man who spoke with a tear in his eye. Now joined – joined together – with a snip and a splice. *Reminded of a little story.* Now for the beat of the timely and the timeless – waves that rise from the ocean floor. *Never looked at it that way.* I have a hundred New-foundland waves, but none is the sound I am looking for. Grumbling my prob-lem to a TV producer. Why don't you check the waves that are stored in the audio-vault? There's every kind of wave that's heard on earth. *The value of life.* Borrowing waves heard by other humans at other times. Waves of a month or so ago – taped for a Darwin documentary – recorded in the Galapagos by the CBC. *You draw strength.* Waves that Darwin knew but didn't hear. What could be more appropriate than waves continuously falling on other shores?

Chapter 14

The come-back – the come-back – the come-back. I hear the voice of the comely Siren. Touting a placid island in stormy seas.

A decrepit old concert-pianist is led out onto a stage.

I hear a voice among the music – the voice of the Siren who won't stop calling. Dollars are floating in the air, Glenn. As thick as the leaves on the trees. You can gather up dollars in baskets, Glenn. Watch the storms while standing on shore. I hear the beckoning Siren – I paddle nearer so I can see. A croaking voice, a flowing robe and a silly wig. Just an actor playing a role. But wait a minute! – wait a minute! What is this? The persona behind the mask of the Siren – turns out to be me!

To make

A boy dancing in the midst of a crowd.
A sculptor re-creating himself in stone.
A voice at the other end of a phone.

of the self

What do you think of this theory of displacement?
That people are leading lives that they don't feel that they were born to lead?
That they have been thwarted and are walking on a less-desired path?

one's magnum opus.

An island surrounded by stormy seas.
A nest of fledglings taking flight.
A train filled with soldiers off to war.

An agreement with CBC Radio.
A beggar holding out a tin cup.

Access to the CBC studios. Engineers and equipment. To create a major documentary every year. To edit the radio-tapes in my own studio. To deliver the finished product to the CBC. Complete freedom to choose whatever topics I fancy. To develop my own form for every program. I yield on money – I am practically working for free – but I will be doing what it pleases me to do.

At last, the virtuoso showed signs of approaching old age. Certain passages became too difficult. Aches and pains restricted his range. Fewer people came to see him. Managers frowned as they counted the heads in the concert halls.

"The radio programs have the polish which comes from hours and hours of focused work."

"Glenn Gould operates at the top of every field of endeavour to which he applies himself."

I am somewhere in Asia! Around me there are mountains with mist on the hillsides! There are rice paddies and peasants at work in the fields! I know that I am in China, but I don't know why! A crowd in the centre of a mountain village! The villagers form a circle in an open space! I cannot see past the people, but I know what they behold! In the centre is a boy and a man who is playing a flute!

What to squeeze in-between - reconsidering my approach - any wish you might like - lost on a mountain - reading me the reviews - a jar with a lid on top - trapped underneath the piano - the biggest gain - the listener is serious - haven't been myself.

The day I quit the concert-circuit? There wasn't any such day. Nor was there a sentimental farewell tour.

I simply appeared in public less and less. In fact, I made a joke. I said that I didn't very often attend concerts – not even my own.

The need for them had simply faded away. I had gotten what I wanted from them. I simply decided that it was time to make the change.

"I should have made my instructions more specific!
I meant that he should roll the rock – uphill!"

A phone call from out of the blue. A phone call from France. A young TV director named Monsaingeon.

A shipwrecked sailor washing up on shore.

A young man with an idea. A way to make television work. A way to express his sense of music on TV. Wants to work with me on programs. Feels we think a lot alike. Wants to get away from the stodgy and the dull. Insists on flying here to Toronto. Wants to show me what he's done. Do Canadians ever watch European TV? Will my cassettes be able to play on your equipment?

One day he was told that he had been cured. Free to go out into the world. No longer dependent on breathing the mountain air. Free to live the life that perhaps he had been born to live. Free to choose a life from among all those on display.

Shovelling a pile of money into a mud-puddle.
Sitting down to play on my rickety chair.

The boy is three years old! Dressed in traditional Chinese garb! He is dancing to the music of the flute! He is dancing in a way that amazes me! Water assuming form when poured into a jar – a jar assuming form when water is poured! Is the boy becoming the music or is the music becoming the boy? I ask the man how the boy can dance in this way!

Does he weave himself - imperturbable self-reliance - take our lumps and bumps - a pause in a youthful journey - our mixing-bowl - freedom from the burden - the bleeding is all inside - his freedom to soar - face that fact - a little gem.

Chicks know when to hatch. Fledglings know when to fly. People are similar, but they often lack the nerve.

What was going to pay the bills? Would my recordings continue to sell? Would I miss the commercial advantages of the concert stage?

No, it wasn't particularly heroic. It was a calculated risk. No performer had ever existed by recordings alone.

I didn't want to continue – so I didn't. I wanted to quit – so I did. There are times when one is completely in harmony with oneself.

"Go back down and make your music where you came from.
Despite your gifts, you have failed to understand.
The demons are the reason for the music.
Without the demons there could be no music at all."

Taping the Mennonite community in Manitoba. A contrapuntal radio-documentary. My autobiography by displacement.

A little boy looking at the world through a paper mask.

The quiet in the land. The calm at the heart of the frenzy. The building that stands when all others collapse in a storm. In the world – but not of the world. A possibility of quadraphonic sound. *Always at arm's length.* A cast of nine. A Mennonite service. Shuttlecock and battledore. Voices chirping – voices weeping. Voices crowing – voices afraid. *Relating to people.* Solitude and isolation – creativity at cost. An island of religion in a secular world – an island as an idea amidst an ocean of competing ideas. Sometimes the waters are choppy – sometimes the waters are smooth. Sometimes the ferry does not connect at all. *Encounters with the world.* Spirituality – materialization. Brooding cello – wailing voice. Janis Joplin meets Johann Sebastian Bach. *Concentrate on a few things in life and do them well.* Layers and layers of concerned voices – voices crying out in the wilderness. Have you seen a Mercedes Benz that can pull a plough?

Glenn Gould Plays Bach: The English Suites Complete / Suite No. 1 in A Major, BWV 806 / Suite No. 2 in A Minor, BWV 807 / Suite No. 3 in G Minor, BWV 808 / Suite No. 4 in F Major, BWV 809 / Suite No. 5 in E Minor, BWV 810 / Suite No. 6 in D Minor, BWV 811 / Hindemith: Das Marienleben for Soprano & Piano / Das Marienleben / Bach: The Toccatas, Vol. 1 / Toccata in F-sharp minor, BWV 910 / Toccata in D major, BWV 912 / Toccata in D minor, BWV 913 / Bach: The Toccatas, Vol. 2 / Toccata in C minor, BWV 911 / Toccata in E minor, BWV 914 / Toccata in G minor, BWV 915 / Toccata in G major, BWV 916 /

Perfection is now a possibility for a performer. I suffered agonies in performance – every note was important to me – I wanted the listener to hear exactly what I could hear. Now I can work all night in the studio in pursuit of the elusive ideal. A week to get thirty-eight minutes of perfect sound. All I want is to give the very best of Glenn Gould.

> *A blind man playing organ music.*
> *A pianist soaking his hands in hot water.*
> *A Greek hero rolling a rock uphill.*

How much of himself to reveal \ the sequential nonsequiturs \ their mutually complimentary interval relationships \ time-transcending objective \ redefined the role \ the altar of cadential affirmation \ the occasional flirtations with gravity \ the emotional tenor of any moment \ a fundamental coordinating intelligence \ repose at the core of his being.

Were you born to be a composer?
Has that been your failed career?
Have you had to seek out other means of being creative?

But the boy was very unhappy.

> *A climber walking down a mountainside.*
> *Water being poured into a jar.*

Children playing and laughing in a schoolyard.

"Of course, the hands are the biggest worry. Will the hands give out too soon? I know he talks about retiring. No more recordings after age fifty and that kind of talk. My guess is that Glenn will keep making music as long as he can."

A meeting with Monsaingeon. He has flown in from Paris to explain what he has in mind. I tell him that I am wary of TV.

Two steely-eyed chess-players, face to face at high noon.

Monsaingeon outlines his terms and I outline mine. My every second thought is control, control, control. Location, finances, schedule, technical standards, number of programs, topics of programs, format of programs, broadcast rights, distribution – the only thing I don't mention is Glenn Gould's fee. What is the essence of the enterprise? What is each of us trying to achieve? Who will control the final product? How much Monsaingeon and how much Glenn Gould will there be? The project shapes itself as we talk. He produces a treasure-trove and hands me the key. Inside I find what I want – heaps of control upon heaps of control. Money from Munich – filming in Toronto – editing in Paris. He is to do what he does well – all the rest will be left to me. He understands when I tell him why I never shake hands.

He watched the girl as she watched her cousin pulling out of the station. Her indifference as hundreds of young men's faces went by. Japanese soldiers sent to Manchuria to fight and to die. Suddenly! – the Soldier of Fortune! – on the very same train! A stricken O-Nami as the rest of the train moved by!

"Glenn Gould gives us voices on top of voices on top of voices."
"What an impossible world if everyone talked at once."

He asks the boy to stand still! He places his hands on the limbs of the boy! He moves the boy in many ways! The boy is placed in intricate poses! The life goes out of the boy and into the man! – the life goes out of the man and into the boy! The boy is dancing and being danced! The man is the boy and not the boy! – the boy is the man and not the man! Each one moves and each is being moved! When the man removes his hands, the boy continues on! The flute is heard before the man resumes the playing! The boy becomes the music becomes the dance!

This noise is going on - been burned to a crisp - best keep silent - the topic is always - surface without a core - the mirror-image of the other - further and further north - always know the direction - he offers his music - a single kayak.

So – let's see – what finally happened? I concentrated more on making recordings. I concentrated less on playing concerts.

I suffered more and more at the thought of giving public recitals. Some I was forced to cancel. Some I cancelled without excuse.

Finally, I cancelled an appearance in Minneapolis. I assured my manager that I would make it up sometime. The days went by and I got busy and it finally dawned on me that I would never play the piano in public again.

> *When the archer*
> *fired the arrow,*
> *his back was exposed.*

Recording in English and German. Winnipeg and Waterloo.
A line of horses and buggies outside a country church.

A cast of interweaving voices. Voices loud – voices soft. The children playing in the schoolyard – the adults praying in the church. The ostinato – the basso continuo – of the train and the water on the rock. *Faced with problems and pressures.* People will say, I am sure, that they cannot hear every word of every speaker. They will concentrate on the surface and not the depths. The tone of every voice is entirely sincere. The interweaving of the voices will be the point. *A way of life that has meaning.* Each voice leads a life of its own. A life in harmony – a life in conflict. All for one – all for none. Each person as a note in a larger symphony – each person as a symphony all its own. *You work at your destiny.* Do we make shelter from the trees of our forests? Do we make food from the plants in our fields? Do we make fire from the sparks of the lightning? Do we make altars from the mud beneath our feet? A response to life from the materials of life itself.

That Bach was valued as a cobbler or a tailor. That his living conditions were dismal and dark. That an operation on his eyesight had failed. That he was nearly paralyzed. That he continued writing the music that everyone shunned.

Playing when there is no one else to hear me.
Sending records out to cleanse the atmosphere.

A phone call to a friend.

"So how about this? Let's try it on for size. We are back quite a ways in the past. Some time in the Middle Ages. A cathedral is being built. A stonemason is chipping away at a block of stone. Once in a while, he puts his tools down and walks to the water-trough. He doesn't take a drink. He looks down at the water and then walks back and picks up his tools and continues to chip away. This will be me, he thinks to himself. This will be me, but no one who knows me will ever know. These are my ears, but bigger ears. This is my nose, but a much longer nose. This is my forehead, but broader and fuller than the one that I see. You know gargoyles have a purpose. They are not just for decoration. Not many people seem aware of that fact. Every so often, the stone-mason pauses. He puts down his hammer and chisel. He walks across the courtyard to the water-trough. He looks down at the water for a while. 'Admiring yourself?' calls the master-mason, tossing a stone-chip into the trough. 'Not likely,' the stone-mason chuckles, without shifting his gaze. He watches the ripples as his features slip and slide on the miniature waves. Proportion and distortion – the game is the same. The mason strolls back to the block of stone and starts in again. And my mouth – oh what a mouth. More like a trumpet than a human face. A trumpet calling to the faithful on sacred days. A change of chisel and shorter strokes as the day goes by. This gargoyle will represent me, though no one will ever know. Every outward feature distorted and twisted each way."

Only saw one road - weighing the challenges - theory of displacement - distorted and twisted - every note was important - all the biographies - new plans - the puzzle of the self - oracular pronouncements - the silence of being.

I decided that I would make the best recorded music of which I was capable. I would use all available resources to that end. I would make as many recordings as I could.

I would study as much music as time permitted. I would put my personal stamp on every piece. Present the voice in which the music spoke to me.

I would do so without regard to consequences. Praise or blame would be irrelevant, you see. The music itself would tell me how well I had played.

The little bird
went soaring
across the sky.

Monsaingeon is a joy to work with. Presenting sound in a visual medium. Translating classical music into the language of TV.
A little boy striking poses in a fun-house mirror.
This is Glenn Gould through a filter. This is Glenn Gould through a lens. This is the best that he can give you. This is the essence of Glenn Gould. All of the dross is burnt away. Only the head and the fingers survive. Half-way between the earth and the sun. Ecstasy expressed in the black and white of a keyboard – a glass of skim milk and an arrowroot cookie on the side.

"Glenn Gould has produced a significant body of work."
"He could never have done so while riding the merry-go-round."

The water
wears
the rock.

An aging virtuoso taking the stage.
A Siren calling out to sailors at sea.
A pianist holding up a perfect note.

The rock
resists
the water.

Do you see yourself as an interpretive-musician?
Is that a legitimate claim to a place in the musical world?
Is that your best-possible gift to the rest of humankind?

Which intends
to be here
when the other is gone?

Contrapuntal radio. Cutting and splicing tape – the juxtaposition of disparate notes – motif and counter-motif.
The fingers of a diver searching for pearls.
No – one cannot make sense of one listen. Better listen to it twice. Do you float on the surface or do you swim in your life? *Need these kind of crutches.* Ordering of phrase – modulation of cadence. *Remember the child you are.* No, I am not a religious convert – religion is not what this documentary is about. It is a mood-piece, reflective and poetic. *From a mountain, from a tree, from a star.* Listen to it ten times over – listen to it ten times ten. Pick a voice and follow it along. Not a coherent series of statements – coherent statements are the babble. The sounds of the voices are the sense – the contrapuntal simultaneity is the point. *Look at it with that kind of eye.* In the world and of the world. Of the world not in the world. In the world not of the world. Amen.

Chapter 15

A reporter from *People* magazine. He has tracked me down by phone. When am I going to make my comeback? Rumour has it that I will return to the music-scene. He wants anecdotes about the hat and the gloves on stage.

A squirming fish at the other end of the line.

He catches me in a mood and I start to talk. I tell him things about which his voice is implying that he doesn't have an interest. And his voice is also implying that his readers don't have an interest and that he will never bother to tell them about what I am saying. And my voice is implying that I know that he has no interest, and I know that his readers have no interest, but that I – I! – Glenn Gould! – have an interest! – a burning, raging interest! And I'm telling you because they interest me!

To produce art

A painter sketching out a new idea.
A man with bars across his face.
A book with every page left blank.

of the most luminous

What of these wounds that some people believe that you have suffered?
All those lumps and bumps you took in the musical world?
Perhaps some internal-scars that only you would know?

and inspiring order.

A man sitting alone in a diner.
A boy in a military uniform.
A briefcase filled with coloured pills.

Working on an article. Arnold Schoenberg – a Perspective. Trying to get a grip on what Schoenberg means to me.

A man sitting at a piano in the first rays of dawn.

A lecture hall in Los Angeles. A sprinkling of people in the audience. Contemporary Composers and Their Works. Mr. Schoenberg sits and waits for things to start. *Haunted and tortured him.* Mr. Schoenberg stands at the microphone. He speaks, but isn't heard. The man who introduced him stands up and adjusts the microphone. *The breath of other planets.* Mr. Schoenberg clears his throat. He holds up a piece of paper. An advertisement from a newspaper – roughly torn. It cannot be read from this distance. Perhaps he'll tell us what he assumes we are able to read. *What suffering could mean.* Mr. Schoenberg clears his throat. He leans towards the microphone. I wonder sometimes who I am. He turns and looks at the article. He begins to read out loud. *The determination to stand or fall.* 'Theoretician and controversial musical figure' – 'known for the influence' – 'brought to bear on modern music.' *They will know who I am.* Mr. Schoenberg seems out of breath. He pauses and then he clears his throat and says, I thought I was composing for different reasons. He pauses once again. Everybody in the audience sits and waits.

He had made no innovations. Played the music that was handed down. Faithful to every notation – true to the original score. People sighed as they watched him decline. While he could play, he was always welcome in every town.

"Glenn Gould is revolutionizing the form of the radio-documentary."
"If they'd let him, he would do the same for TV."

"Here's something that I imagine Glenn Gould thinks about, though he never confides in me. But it's something that every pianist faces some day. It's that the human body is a machine – a magnificent machine, to be sure – but a machine that is subject to wear and decay. You can hear it on some of the more recent recordings. Short passages where he isn't quite himself. Oh, he can substitute a better note – or a bar or a longer passage – but he can only splice into a piece what he can still play. Read about any older pianist – it's in all the biographies. The hand-eye coordination begins to break down. The span of the hand becomes more restricted. The most demanding passages come to look harder and harder to play. There are sections that your younger self used to relish in your hey-day, but that now you approach with a fear that this won't be your day. Glenn is forty-nine years old. He might be an exception to the general rule – some people seem to age on a different scale. And some days an older performer might find the old limberness has returned. For a person who works with recordings, this would allow him to pick and choose his days to perform. I'm sure he thinks about all this – whether he worries is another affair. Some people move into old age gracefully – for others it's not that way. Imagine a very public contest between Glenn's older and younger selves. I hear he's preparing to tackle the Goldberg again."

The midst of a carnival - simply known as bach - a chance to re-pack - made you what you are - you can do no wrong - the bijoux in the window - absorbed them into my bloodstream - develop recording techniques - of what the human being consists - who will want to listen.

The days are pleasant for me now. So too the nights. I am a creature who thrives on routine.

I eat the same food each day. I rise at about the same time. You could picture me on a turntable, circling around.

At times I phone a friend. We talk – or at least I do. I have some very patient friends who will listen to me.

When the clouds cleared,
the paint
had washed away.

A notepad and a pencil. Thinking and jotting down ideas. Some liner-notes for an album. A Tale of Two Marienlebens.
A car picking up a hitchhiker on a northern road.
So interesting to me that Hindemith would re-write a youthful work. The youthful sprig and the stately tree – the playful puppy and the grizzled dog. V*ery different concepts*. Two realizations of a single work – a quarter-century apart. The writing of notes to tell which version he prefers. *Lifelong quest.* A drawing room in Frankfort. A young man comes to call. Yes, the master is at home. Invited into the study. Please allow me to take your hat and your coat. *The whole cycle.* The young man sits and plays. The youthful Hindemith plays the Marienlebens – the first. All the dash and the panache of a young pianist of twenty-five. All the energy of the leaves that sprout on the trees. He forgets that the old man is in the room. *Provide a proper conclusion.* The old man sits and plays. The aging Hindemith plays the Marienlebens – the second. He is aware that the leaves are falling, but he doesn't take his eyes off the listening youth. *Something had to be overcome.* The old man stops playing. The sound of the music dies away. Each one is about to speak, but the maid appears. Tea and sandwiches will be served on the summer porch.

As soon as he could, he joined the army, as his cousin had done before. Muskets and mini-balls – bayonets and swords. Wearing a uniform – marching in file. Offering one's life for a righteous cause. Booming cannons blowing horses and men in the air.

Remembering the apprentice who spent two years at the family cottage. Remembering the stripling who made his New York debut.

"At times, Glenn seems to be getting quite old. I only see him once in a while, and every time I see him, it's another Glenn Gould. He's a young boy or he's an old man, but I never know which one he's going to be. Once I saw him, and it seemed to be a lull in his creative life. He looked lifeless, old and tired. 'I've recorded everything there is to record. I think I'll stop playing the piano when I'm fifty.' – that sort of thing. Stooped over – a shuffling walk – slumping down in a chair and giving a sigh. 'I've done my work. I'm all played out. I'm so very tired.' And then the next thing you know, when you see him a few months later, he'll be young and boyish again – the Glenn Gould who burst with such freshness upon the world. Much more colour in his face – sparkling eyes and that Glenn-Gould laugh. And he'll be eager to tell you all about his new plans."

Never met a giant - battered and bleeding - i try to remember - rode through a rainstorm - the listener's role - the diplomacy of a dove - searching among the leaves - chasing a floating bubble - lose their sense of themselves - the pilot's taking it in.

I listen to music – the old and the new. I spend many hours preparing a score. The kind of work I do can't be done in a crowd.

I spend much of my time up North, in the small towns along the shore of Lake Superior. I sit in diners and listen to voices. I drive for endless hours in my car.

I no longer have the cottage. I no longer have a dog. I have simplified my life as time has gone by.

"Yes he does,"
said one of his voices.
"The dog knows
exactly who you are."

Peter Ostwald comes to see me. He casually makes a remark. He is writing a book on – Robert Schumann!
Gold-leaf printing on a wall of leather-bound books.
I browbeat him – just a little. Peter! Peter! Peter! Why on Schumann? What a waste! A truly inferior musician! Such dreary compositions! What a shameful misuse of ink and paper! Not even a competent pianist! A failed composer made famous by a clever wife! Oh, Peter! Peter! Peter! What you should do, my Peter, is write a book on a truly important musician! Peter doesn't say a word. His brow furrows and he waits for the storm to subside. I don't say another word. I let it subside.

Bach: Prelude, Fughettas & Fugues / Prelude And Fugue in A minor,
BWV 895 / Prelude And Fughetta in D minor, BWV 899 / Prelude And Fugue

in E minor, BWV 900 / Preludes, BWV 902 & 902A / Fughetta in G major, BWV 902 / Prelude in C major, BWV 924 / Prelude in D major, BWV 925 / Prelude in D minor, BWV 926 / Prelude in F major, BWV 927 / Prelude in F major, BWV 928 / Prelude in G minor, BWV 930 / Prelude in C major, BWV 933 / Prelude in C minor, BWV 934 / Prelude in D minor, BWV 935 / Prelude in D major, BWV 936 / Prelude in E major, BWV 937 / Prelude in E minor, BWV 938 / Fugue in C major, BWV 952 / Fugue in C major, BWV 953 / Fughetta in C minor, BWV 961 /

But the king of all this theory – the amateur-musician-auditor-king – will be the listener. He of the mind – he of the eye – he of the ear. He will not be confined to the offerings of the local concert hall. He will have every recording of every piece of music that has ever been recorded up to the moment of listening pleasure. He will have every sound in the world right there in his room.

An article in a celebrity-gossip magazine.
An older man and a younger man in a room.
A person speaking into a microphone.

The organic application of dissonance \ the mental imagery \ the transcendence of his art \ the meaning of experience \ an attempt to demythologize \ one surpassingly affecting moment \ the superb contrapuntal interplay \ some ultimate transformational impulse \ pretensions to self-sufficiency \ the ratio of cinema to verité.

Have set-backs made you what you are?
Are they barriers you just pushed past?
Have they had any effect on the music that you have made?

He was like a bird in a cage.

Two pieces of tape spliced together.
A quiet man with a furrowed brow.
A person trying on a brand-new crown.

"Glenn is showing signs of aging. Well, none of us gets to keep our looks. The boyishly-slender physique is gone. The toll of pills and sedentary living. Of course, Glenn has a well-known disdain for exercise. Why wouldn't he make his health a major priority? You don't suppose he's willing himself to die?"

Toronto City Hall. The Council Chamber. I sit in the makeshift theatre. A preview of my film, Glenn Gould's Toronto.
I'm ready for my close-up, Mister DeMille.
A young representative of the Mayor. A couple of workmen make one

last adjustment to the temporary screen. A special showing – just for me alone. *Find a certain tranquillity.* Tomorrow night, the official viewing will be held. Limousines and taxis – tuxedos and elegant gowns. Toronto's finest will come to see an homage to their town. *The peace that the earth cannot give.* The next day, the reviewers will be furious. Gallons of vitriolic bile. *Metaphoric stained-glass window.* Their complaint will be that Glenn Gould wasn't there! *Controlled by my memory.* Alone in the makeshift theatre. Just myself and the young assistant. *Nothing more than a mirage.* No popcorn, but if there was, I wouldn't eat it. *If that mirage were ever to evaporate.* The lights go down – the screen lights up. And here am I – Glenn Gould – thirty feet high!

Finally, the painter knew that he could paint her. The answer to the mystery had been revealed. He knew now what had been missing all along. He knew now what had been holding the girl together. He would paint what he now knew the girl to be.

"Pianists are replaceable units – they wear out like a record or a phonograph."

"A new crop of good young pianists is required in classical music about every twenty years."

"I have the ultimate, mother-of-all-mothers theory of the enigma that everyone sees in the long-pursued but ever-elusive Glenn Gould. Yes, I admit that he appears to be extremely exotic – the artist as creative-angel, who lives in a world beyond the realm of the normal human being, in an extremely remote and rarified atmosphere. The 'artiste' who breathes only oxygen – clean and pure. Sure he's the man who became the darling of the concert-circuit, at the virtuoso-age of twenty-three – who walked away from the adulation – who locks himself in a studio at midnight, studies music and puts out records year after year – who lives alone, for the most part – who phones people up and does a monologue at all hours of the night. The man who resists psychological probing – who shuts himself off from his parents and family and friends – the one who drives further North each time he gets in his car. But look at him closely and what do you see? The secret to Glenn Gould is that there is no escape. Life is the same at the farthest poles. You are never far away from the blood in your veins. So – Glenn's music is the unusual in the usual – the complexity in the every-day familiar – the new sound each time you hear the same music again. For all his genius – because of his genius – for all his affectations – for all his quirks of personality and behaviour – Glenn Gould is just a living and breathing, drinking and eating, working and sleeping, laughing and crying, enjoying and suffering – as every-day-as-you-or-me – human being."

Trainload of cattle-cars - missed-out-on-life - the essential glenn gould - made a great find - tainted by stale ideas - the girl in the painting - pil-

grimages to sacred sights - a day when you know - to give his music a name - in the cockpit.

Often, I spend my nights in a recording studio. In fact, I am busy making a new recording now. The Goldberg Variations.

Yes, the Goldberg Variations. I first recorded it when I was twenty-three. And now I am approaching fifty, and now I am recording it again.

So what will be the same and what will be different? Well, what is the same in me will be the same. And what is different in me will be different.

> *But not one moment*
> *since it was a seed*
> *had been lost to the tree.*

Jotting down notes for a review. Geoffrey Payzant's new book. Glenn Gould: Music and Mind.

A technician placing a slide on a microscope.

Jotting phrases down as I read. *Communication entirely on his own terms.* Less of the childhood would have been better. *How much of himself to reveal.* Very little of the life and times. *How much to keep secret.* A skilful study of the themes and counter-themes. *The rites of passage between notes.* A word or two about ecstasy and inwardness. *Media manipulation.* The absence of a question-and-answer interchange with its ostensible subject, Glenn Gould. *Clear-eyed detachment.* Structurally secure and chromatically complex – what more could a mouse in a laboratory ask? *Conventional image of Gould.* A room in a northern motel. Voices chat in the parking lot. Glenn Gould reviewing a book about Glenn Gould.

"Well, I must thank this fellow, Bach. I will send him a gift of gold. A golden goblet containing one hundred Louis d'or. But even so, I shall still be in his debt. For my affliction music has been the only cure."

Remembering the boy who would practice until his hands would bleed.

Remembering the child on the rug in Uptergrove.

"What kind of man is Glenn Gould? Well, I'll tell you, I don't know him very well, but here's a story that was told to me by someone else. Not the person in the story, no, but told to him, in a roundabout way, by a person who was there. The story was told to me in a little Italian restaurant in Toronto. Lasagna – and a very good lasagna it was – and set off with a very good local-neighbourhood Italian red wine. This person – a studio technician or an electrician or whatever it was – he was working in the studio one night and they were all taking a break. And this fellow – this maybe-electrician – hummed a tune.

Asked his boss what it was. Was it something this fellow – this piano-fellow, this Glenn Gould – might be able to play? Just a bit of classical music he had in his head. Well, none of them was in awe of Glenn Gould – they were just the technical staff. So this fellow – this electrician – he hums these notes to Glenn Gould. He was sitting at the piano when they all got back. Probably a drink of bottled water and a couple of arrowroot cookies. 'It's Chopin', said Glenn Gould, to this fellow. 'Normally it's something I would avoid, but if you like this piece, I'll see what I can do.' Then – according to my informant – I got this second-hand – Glenn starts to work with these few notes. Improvising on the spot. Ten minutes of splendid music. The electrician just stood there wide-eyed. Just a few notes and look at what this piano-guy can do! So when Glenn Gould finished, the electrician thanked him and held out his hand. Well, now you're waiting for the punch-line. Do you think Glenn Gould shook the little guy's hand or not? Anyway, the actual punch-line is a question: does this tell you anything about Glenn Gould? – or not? I got all this from someone else, as I told you, so I can't, in all honesty, swear that it's true."

Followed that trajectory - questions about how they manage - a nest of fledglings - a face reflected - measured by a yardstick - the elusive ideal - allow him to pick and choose - many hours preparing - bring it under control - every outward feature.

So my life has come full-circle. I fell in love with recording. I recorded the Goldberg Variations.

I didn't like performing. I retired from performing. I studied and recorded the music that appealed to me.

Now I am recording the Goldberg Variations again. What goes around comes around. Who says one cannot swallow one's own tail?

"Does eternity not mean
that all things have existence
simultaneously?"

There is never enough time to read. I have made myself out of the recycled pages of many books.

A finger slowly moving across a page.

I often muse that it would be interesting to have one book on my wall of books which has only blank pages. I would take it down and peruse it once in a while. Perhaps a date on every page. Beginning on the day of my birth. A new date could be added every day. Not a diary – not something to write in – but a book which always remains a blank-page book. The thought, as the book is perused, would be of the life that is being led that is never – ever – going to be written down. Snap the blank-book shut and return it to the shelf.

"Glenn Gould will be a famous pianist long after he and all of his contemporaries are long dead."

"People will point to him as the light at the top of the hill."

When the land
is dry
as dust

A man slumping down on a chair.
A person explaining the finer points of a theory.
An aging pianist massaging his stiffening hands.

all the
pretty petals
fade

Why do you play-down the life – both yours and others?

Why do you play-up the music – of others and yourself?

Isn't the life pretty much the same as the music – isn't the music pretty much the same as the life?

and the plant
with the deepest roots
continues to flower.

A bit of ennui and a need for renewal. I am forty-nine years old. I have come a long way on the path that I have blazed.

A boy and a dog walking through the woods.

A sense that the time is short, for me, as it is for everyone. The baby in the crib hears the chimes of the clock. I have said that I expect to die at fifty. Once I joked that I would live to one hundred and six. I am not enthralled with the mirror, but I respect what it reveals. Slightly bald and a middle-age paunch – aches and pains in the back and the knees – stiffening joints in the Glenn-Gould hands. Strategic losses for sure, but the brain is still as sharp as Excalibur. Muffled shouts from the parking lot. Teenagers down below in the falling snow – taking turns shooting a puck at the net. What to do with whatever time is left to me? Sitting here in my studio. Rows of books and a shelf of records. Total silence and the lights down low. A cup of tea and an arrowroot cookie. Speakers facing me in the twilight. Waiting for the well to fill again.

Chapter 16

Listening to myself at twenty-three. The Goldberg Variations.
Two people listening as a record turns round and round.
Not completely pleased with what I find. A rather spooky experience. Like meeting myself on a road somewhere north of Superior. Do I step on the gas or stop and pick him up? A great pleasure in many respects. My fingerprints are still visible on the surface, but I am not the person who made this recording any more. Some other person is locked within these grooves. A little bit immature. A student noodling while his teacher is out of the room. Quite a bit of piano-playing going on. The best that was in the boy I used to be.

It has been said

Newspaper articles hailing a young phenomenon.
People sitting and waiting in a hall.
A young stripling coming out on stage.

that the greatest puzzle of every life

Who are you?
What are you?
What do you want to be?

is the puzzle of the self.

A stagehand adjusting the height of a piano.
A young boy wearing a hat and winter gloves.
An audience getting restless in their seats.

On the train. From Toronto to New York.
A face reflected in the window of a train.
On the road from twenty-three to forty-nine. What I was and what I am – what I have lost and what I have gained. A wave in the rear-view mirror

on a northern road. Months of thinking, experimenting, considering. What I know now that I didn't know back then. Months of thought and deliberation. Years of learning how to play. Bach is still the ultimate challenge, as he has always been. Glenn Gould 1 and Glenn Gould 2 – Glenn Gould multiplied by Glenn Gould. On my way to record the Goldberg once again.

After he died, he was largely forgotten. Others came to take his place. Always a new, young concert-virtuoso. A current toast of the musical scene. Occasionally, an older person would visit his grave.

"I don't know why he wants to go back and record the Goldberg again."
"Well, maybe he thinks he's got something new to say."

A hand is gently shaking my shoulder! I flinch and hope that no damage has been done! I open my eyes and look around me! I am seated in an aeroplane! So it was the drone of the engines that made it so hard to sleep! The stewardess bends and whispers! She looks calm, but her voice has an anxious twinge! "Excuse me, Sir, but a lady a few rows back has told me that you were a fighter-pilot during the war! We have an emergency and we badly need your help! Our pilot and our co-pilot have unfortunately succumbed to food poisoning! They are both lying unconscious on the cockpit floor! We are flying on auto-pilot! We need you desperately to take the controls of the plane!"

Whose face is obscured - pleased himself to write - a moment's peace - when everything changed - the most loathsome recording - errors clogging their grooves - a celebrity cast in wax - break the bounds - saw his own skeleton - serve the dance.

So that's it. These are some of what have been labelled as the 'traumatic moments' in my life. These are the moments at which, people speculate, I have felt life most intensely.

Childhood – Competition – Cottage. Russia – Hamburg – Desert. Bernstein – Hupfer – Szell.

The Goldberg – the Life – the Goldberg. Stepping stones and stumbling blocks. A string of worry beads – light and dark.

I could go on, I suppose. More beads could be spitted onto the skewer. I assume that's what you want me to do.

Every day
the little boy
sat at the piano.

Seeking out a new piano. A new person should have a new instrument to play. The Steinways all seek to evoke the old Glenn Gould.

A display in the window of a music store.

How about a Steinway made in Germany, Sir? How would the Bechstein sound suit you, Mr. Gould? I've heard some Yamahas on recordings that have left me pleased. The Ostrovsky Piano Company. Opposite Carnegie Hall. By arrangement with Mrs. Ostrovsky. She has sheets hung up like a wall across the front window. You can hear, but cannot see, the next Glenn Gould. Not the sound I had hoped to hear. A quick 'merci' on my way to the door. But there – in a neglected corner, battered and bruised, like my old friend at the cottage. I try a few notes and am delightfully intrigued by the sound. Please ship this to Columbia Studios on East 30th Street. The Glenn Gould that you will hear will be brand-new.

Dodge a bullet, think a thought, then dodge one again. If he died, would that be the end? If he lived, what should he do? What to aspire to – what to shun? How many selves are waiting inside us, still to be born?

Spending long hours rethinking my early recording.
Taking the train down to New York once more.

"But I am not a pilot," I say! "I am a pianist! I can also play the organ and the harpsichord! The man across from me in the aisle was a pilot in the war! This lady must have heard us talking and has made a mistake! We became friendly and I gave him my dinner, as I never eat on a plane! And in any case, fish is far from my favourite food!" "Our problems multiply," the stewardess whispers! "The man across the aisle from you is completely unconscious as well! Our dilemma was caused by a serving of tainted fish! If you gave him your dinner, as you tell me you have done, then you have poisoned the pilot – though inadvertently!"

To meet the mark - the music that we enjoy - the brightest glow - burying the demons - insist on hearing the worst - like toys on a table top - alive with roots - concentrate on the vision - dwell at the deepest core - i would call a miracle.

But what does all of it mean?, you might ask. Well, I'm sorry, but that's a closed book. Un livre fermé.

To isolate such moments is to go against the music. There have been thousands of such moments along the way. Have you ever wondered how many notes in a fugue?

So this theory of yours is interesting, but I should never have spoken to you, or even let myself daydream in this way. From now on – no more phone calls – not from me – not from you. I won't be phoning you in future and I won't be returning your calls.

*He would practice
until his fingers
would bleed.*

Columbia Studios again. East 30th Street in Manhattan. One of the last recordings to be made before they tear this old place down.

A twenty-three year old pianist in scarf and gloves.

My battered Yamaha in place. Up on blocks and freshly-tuned. A last-minute adjustment to my father's chair. Playing one Variation at a time. An entirely new conception of the Goldberg. The relationships of the tempi. The pulse-rate – the rhythmic reference point. Basic pulse and subsidiary pulse – taking a pulse and making it multiply and divide. From four PM until midnight – six days of recording in all. The result of months and months of developing thought – the result of many years of sun and rain. This Goldberg will be the essence of Glenn Gould now. Will this chair hold up for another twenty-six years?

Beethoven: Piano Sonatas, Op. 2, Nos. 1-3, Op. 28, "Pastoral" / Piano Sonata No. 1 / Piano Sonata No. 2 / Piano Sonata No. 3 / Piano Sonata No. 15 / The Glenn Gould Silver Jubilee Album / Scarlatti: Sonatas, L 463, 413, and 486 / C.P.E. Bach: Württemberg Sonata No. 1 / Gould: So You Want to Write A Fugue? / Scriabin: Two Pieces, Op. 57 / Strauss: Ophelia-Lieder / Beethoven-Liszt: Pastoral Symphony, First Movement / A Glenn Gould Fantasy / Haydn: The Six Last Sonatas / Piano Sonata No. 56, Hob. XVI / No. 42 / Piano Sonata No. 58, Hob. XVI / No. 48 / Piano Sonata No. 59, Hob. XVI / No. 49 / Piano Sonata No. 60, Hob. XVI / No. 50 / Piano Sonata No. 61, Hob. XVI / No. 51 / Piano Sonata No. 62, Hob. XVI / No. 52 / Bach: The Goldberg Variations.

And best of all – best of all. All present roles in the musical structure will fade away – they will all blend together into one significant role. The listener will become the composer – the listener will become the performer – the listener will become the technician too. He will re-create the music with his own musical dials. These dials will be his piano, his flugelhorn, his violin. By enhancement, by distortion, by snipping and splicing and so much more – with controls not yet invented, yet soon to come – he will change the music which is offered to him by his fellow musical-artisans to the music that, in his mind, he already hears.

*Loud chatter by patrons in a lobby.
A reporter filing his story on a telephone.
Intense applause as a young man enters a room.*

The rites of passage between notes \ the ultimate composer-performer-

critic-consumer hybrid \ extra-musical mystique \ the known exterior world and the ideal interior world \ the larger purposes of creativity \ mythic anonymity \ measured by a yardstick \ the relevant criterion \ primary cadences of a unique cumulative power and resonance \ the silence of being.

What is the path that you are on?
What is the path that is easy to follow?
What is the path that you feel so compelled to blaze?

Who would rescue this boy if he didn't rescue himself?

Taxis pulling up to a major venue.
A newsboy shouting news of the latest sensation.
A crowd lining up for major event.

As for my health, it's always been a matter of contention between my hypochondria and whatever the state of my health might appear to be. My hands feel quite light and limber these days. Some of the problems that raised concerns have faded away. A long-term trend or a temporary lull? – half-way through or the end of the line? Don't ask if there's a doctor in the house. A hypochondriac's delight at forty-nine.

Working with Monsaingeon. A TV show of the recording session. Though – not exactly.
A camera honing in on a pair of hands.
Playing every Variation through again. One version for the recording and one for the television show. One's requirements would have conflicted with those of the other. The event – and then the event engendered again. Very few will notice the difference. They will vary a note or two. Why should there not be more than one of Glenn Gould? There has been sunshine and there has been rain. Many notes have washed up on the shore. A twenty-three year-old perched on a rock at forty-nine. This is the music that the tide has left behind.

He knew what made her Ophelia and not Ophelia. What had made her mad and what had made her sane. What had made her cruel and what had made her kind. What made her dead and what made her so alive. She was the train and the dagger and those coins.

"The great composers are the gods who are sending their oracular pronouncements down to earth."
"The runner's voice is the only sound that the villagers hear."

"But wait a moment," I say, upon reflection! "Calm is required at a moment like this! Any panic must be dismissed from our thoughts!" The stewardess leads me to the cockpit! I step over the groaning pilot and the suffering co-pilot too! "It's called the Midas Syndrome," I say, as I brush the various controls with my handkerchief! "It is the state of having the confidence that – having had extraordinary success in my primary field of endeavour – I will always be able to achieve a similar level of success in any field to which I choose to turn my attention!" I move the controls on the pilot's seat! I lower it down until my eyes are at the right height! "In short," I tell the stewardess, "it is a sense that one acquires that everything that I touch – in any enterprise whatsoever – will turn to gold!" I place my fingers on the instruments! The feel is not quite right! I ask the stewardess for a hot towel to heat my hands! She releases the auto-pilot and the joystick jumps at my touch! A bit of turbulence, but I bring it under control! "So I have no doubt – whatsoever – that I will be able to successfully fly – and to land, when we reach our goal – this aeroplane!"

Dare to open a window - the-agony-of-the-denied - splicing two pieces of tape - the minefield of his daydreams - a catapult to the heavens - keep it simple - the conversation of a lifetime - coined when you were new - digging a hole - isolation and deprivation.

I will be here – in this room. Playing my records and my tapes. Imagining scores in my head and perfecting my future recordings.

Constantly moving between my apartment and my studio. Constantly moving between Toronto and Northern Ontario. Listening to music on the radio and voices in coffee shops.

Keeping people at a distance. None of them close – not even you. Sending my music to them at intervals, like the pulsing of a distant star.

The black
and the red
and the white
would intermingle.

Back home, again, in Toronto. The second Goldberg is in the can. Now the editing begins.

An iceberg floating silently in northern seas.

Listening to the tapes for days and days. The aim is to make the perfect recording. No mistakes as there are in life. No false-notes as there are in a concert hall. This recording will feature only the best of Glenn Gould. Slumping in an armchair. A cup of tea and an arrowroot cookie. Listening to the play-backs time and again. Considering every single note in its bid to represent me. From each velvet tray – a single perfect offering. From the ocean-bed to its place in my string of pearls. Stretching my mind as far as I can. Wondering how close to the ideal I can come. Sending my edit-requests to New York. Not one sour note will survive me after I die.

The Count now knew a way to summon sleep. The Master was always eager to savour the magic, again and again. He would say, "Dear Goldberg, play me one of my variations." His name for the music which came to him with no name. The Court Musician would play the music far into the night.

Spending long hours working in the studio.
Recording the Goldberg once again.

A phone call to a friend.
"Let's say – just for interest's sake – that there's a boy who lives in the woods. At his parents' cottage, beside a lake. And it's basically a summer location where people come to stay a few weeks and walk the trails and fish and swim and enjoy the scenery. And this boy is a normal boy. He has a head and a body like everyone else. But a strange phenomenon begins to occur. He goes out for walks on the trails. He takes his dog along. Neither leads, as they are so used to one another. They seem to choose each trail simultaneously. But the boy keeps meeting people. And they all make a big fuss. They are all sympathetic, mind you, but they all think that something is wrong. 'Oh you poor boy – such a big head and such a little body! However do you manage to get along?' And then they choose another trail – the boy and the dog – and meet another group of hikers and someone says, 'Oh you poor boy – such a big body and so little head! However do you manage to get along?' So the summer, of course, goes on – and the tourists come and go on the trails – but the boy is always happiest when he is walking alone with his dog. The dog, of course, doesn't know this is going on.
"So – do you think you are getting a glimpse of what I mean?"

Live alone among my fellows - free to choose a life - put my personal stamp - redefined the role - glenn is a must - i have no doubt - long hours re-thinking - the kind of work i do - a very public contest - what the world now knows.

So this is my choice and this is my destiny. The two are in accord. I could not be any happier, whatever some might say.

I function best alone. All I am and all I need be. Just me alone with my music.

With all my listeners way out there. Listening only to the music. Many miles away and many years from now.

Making music
that he could
taste and feel and see.

Editing the television show with Monsaingeon. The television version of the second Goldberg.

A vase filled with blue chrysanthemums.

A department store with a bank of screens. Between the blenders and the waffle irons. A dozen Glenn Goulds playing, with the sound turned low. Shopping specials blare from the speakers. But come a little closer – approach the multiple Glenn Goulds. The music is faint, so you lean in close. The fingers dance across the keys. You are a cleaning lady in Hamburg – you have never heard of Bach. What is every one of these images saying to you?

"I like the early Glenn-Gould recordings – all the promise of the early spring."

"To me – musicians are at their best in their autumn-years."

The nectar
is still dripping
from the petals.

Newspaper stories about a new discovery.
Teenagers lining up with autograph books.
A boy playing a piano all alone.

The dew
is still moist
on the leaves.

Are you there yet?
Are you there yet?
Are you there?

You can go there
if you remember
where it is.

One-thirty in the morning. A drive through Toronto. A taping at a studio downtown.

A baggy-pants vaudevillian with hat and cane.

Drumming up a little publicity. An interview with Tim Page. We talk as he asks me questions. Me with my answers to the questions – Tim with the questions that I have written for him to ask. Glenn Gould being interviewed by Glenn Gould. What the Goldberg means to me – what I felt at twenty-three – what I feel at forty-nine. What the second Goldberg has that the first one lacks. Tim as my alter-ego – me as one of my selves. 'Mr. Gould's questions will be read by Mr. Tim Page.' – 'Glenn Gould will be played by Mr.

Glenn Gould.' I am editing my life as best I can.

A clock glowing dimly on a wall.

Tim goes out to get a drink. A cup of coffee or a soda pop. I see an old piano over in the corner against the wall. I sit down and start to play. Variation Nineteen of the Goldberg. Wish Old Bach could hear me play. I play with just one listener – me alone. Tim comes back with his cup of coffee. He leans against the wall. I stop playing and I look at him. Three-thirty on the studio clock. You know, Tim, these are the happiest days of my life.

Three Books

Glenn Gould: Light and Dark – a novel
Glenn Gould's life as a musician begins as a fairy-tale, as his very first record-ing – the Goldberg Variations – skyrockets the young Canadian to the top of the music world, as a must-see and must-hear concert-pianist with sold-out performances all around the world. And then, at the height of his powers and his popularity, he makes a decision about his music and his life which splits the music world right down the middle, and remains controversial to this day.

The Making of Glenn Gould: Light and Dark – a reflective journal
This journal records the author's reflections on the process of the crafting of the novel as it evolved through the stages of planning, writing, editing and polishing. It constitutes an effort to be as conscious as possible of the process whereby the single idea that suggested the topic of the novel was expanded into a complex work of art. Topics range from the nuts and bolts of novel-building to the nature of the novel as an art-form.

Planning Glenn Gould: Light and Dark – a planning notebook
During the writing of the novel, the author kept a hand-written notebook which records the day-by-day development of the novel as it found its shape and style. The notebook – now in print form – reveals how a vast cluster of thoughts was sifted, selected, structured and polished into novel-form.

The Project
Together, this novel, journal and notebook comprise the twenty-second install-ment in an on-going novel-writing project in which the author is exploring the concept of form and meaning in the novel, and of the novel as a form of expression in the 21st Century. All of the published journals and notebooks are available for free download at www.johnpassfield.ca.

About the Author

John Passfield was born in St. Thomas, Ontario, Canada, and continues to reside in Southern Ontario, near Cayuga, with his family. He is interested in exploring the development of the novel as an art-form, and has written over twenty novels, twenty planning notebooks and twenty journals in his search for a form for the poetic novel of our time. His novel John Passfield: Saturday Morning was shortlisted for the ReLit Award in 2022.

Novels by John Passfield

Grave Song
The Agony of Robert Chisholm

Jumbo
P. T. Barnum's Greatest Creation

Pinafore Park
The Swan Boat Incident

Water Lane
The Pilgrimage of Christopher Marlowe

Rain of Fire
The Ordeal of Conductor Spettigue

Victoria Day
The Fabric of the Community

The Wright Brothers
Flight is Possible

Leni Riefenstahl
The Valley of the Shadow

Babe Ruth
Out of the Park

Raskolnikov
Murder with an Axe

Sergei Eisenstein
Death Day

Albert Einstein
Wonder

Geoffrey Chaucer
Canterbury Bound

Ospringe
A Visit with Grandad

Pompeii
Vesuvius Dominus

Beethoven
The Ninth Immersion

Job
The Cornerstone of the Universe

Bethune
The Only Person Alive in the World

Terry Fox
Somewhere the Hurting Must Stop

Lord and Lady Macbeth
Full of Scorpions Is My Mind

Cyril Passfield
Out West

Glenn Gould
Light and Dark

Emily Brontë
More Myself Than I

L. M. Montgomery
I Gave You Life

Pauline Johnson
Know Who I Am

John Passfield
Saturday Morning

Eleonora Duse
Let Me Have My Wings

James McIntyre
The Mammoth Cheese

Shakespeare and Cleopatra
My Life Is Not My Own

John and Santa
The Cowboy Shirt

John and Cassandra
Fair is Fair

John and Dickens
A Christmas Mystery

John and Lewis Carroll
Wonder Fall

See www.johnpassfield.ca for publishing information.

In Search of Form and Meaning:
Journals by John Passfield

Each journal is a day-by-day record of the complex process that a writer under-goes while crafting a work of art. It records the largest decisions, of structure and theme, and the smallest decisions, such as the choice of one word over another, and the constant interaction between the two. Each journal is a record of a writer's reflection on the craft of novel-writing.

The Making of Grave Song

The Making of Jumbo

The Making of Pinafore Park

The Making of Water Lane

The Making of Rain of Fire

The Making of Victoria Day

The Making of Flight is Possible

The Making of The Valley of the Shadow

The Making of Out of the Park

The Making of Murder with an Axe

The Making of Death Day

The Making of Wonder

The Making of Canterbury Bound

The Making of Ospringe

The Making of Vesuvius Dominus

The Making of The Ninth Immersion

The Making of The Cornerstone of the Universe

The Making of The Only Person Alive in the World

The Making of Somewhere the Hurting Must Stop

The Making of Full of Scorpions Is My Mind

The Making of Out West

The Making of Glenn Gould: Light and Dark

The Making of Emily Brontë: More Myself Than I

The Making of Pauline Johnson: Know Who I Am

The Making of John Passfield: Saturday Morning

The Making of Eleonora Duse: Let Me Have My Wings

The Making of James McIntyre: The Mammoth Cheese

The Making of Shakespeare and Cleopatra: My Life Is Not My Own

The Making of John and Santa: The Cowboy Shirt

The Making of John and Cassandra: Fair is Fair

The Making of John and Dickens: A Christmas Mystery

The Making of John and Lewis Carroll: Wonder Fall

See www.johnpassfield.ca for publishing information.

The Novel as an Art-Form:
Planning Notebooks by John Passfield

Each planning notebook is a printed version of the hand-written notebook which records the planning, writing, editing and polishing of each novel. Each notebook is an attempt to record, understand, and organize the vast cluster of thoughts which occur as one grapples with the various levels of organization which a clear yet complex work of art demands.

Planning Grave Song

Planning Jumbo

Planning Pinafore Park

Planning Water Lane

Planning Rain of Fire

Planning Victoria Day

Planning Flight is Possible

Planning The Valley of the Shadow

Planning Out of the Park

Planning Murder with an Axe

Planning Death Day

Planning Wonder

Planning Canterbury Bound

Planning Ospringe

Planning Vesuvius Dominus

Planning The Ninth Immersion

Planning The Cornerstone of the Universe

Planning The Only Person Alive in the World

Planning Somewhere the Hurting Must Stop

Planning Full of Scorpions Is My Mind

Planning Out West

Planning Glenn Gould: Light and Dark

Planning Emily Brontë: More Myself Than I

Planning L. M. Montgomery: I Gave You Life

Planning Pauline Johnson: Know Who I Am

Planning John Passfield: Saturday Morning

Planning Eleonora Duse: Let Me Have My Wings

Planning James McIntyre: The Mammoth Cheese

Planning Shakespeare and Cleopatra: My Life Is Not My Own

Planning John and Santa: The Cowboy Shirt

Planning John and Cassandra: Fair is Fair

Planning John and Dickens: A Christmas Mystery

Planning John and Lewis Carroll :Wonder Fall

See www.johnpassfield.ca for publishing information.